Rules to Die By

A Matthew Diggerson Mystery

by

D. G. Gillespie

For information, email **Cozy Cat Press**, cozycatpress@aol.com or visit our website at: www.cozycatpress.com

COZY CAT
PRESS

ISBN: 978-1-946063-20-5

Printed in the United States of America

Cover design by Paula Ellenberger
www.paulaellenberger.com

1 2 3 4 5 6 7 8 9 10

Dedicated to the memory of my sweet "Simba" and to the support of Elena, my sweet wife.

Chapter One: Active Verbs

If you want to improve your sentences, their clarity and flow, then here's the best advice you will ever get: Avoid weak-verb phrasing—if you can. Instead, use action verbs, words that create mental pictures, that help readers to understand and to remember, that tighten up your statements and allow you to combine sentences. To-be verbs, like "is" and "are," just link other words together, oftentimes long and awkward word groups, too. Therefore, when you see a word like "is" or "was," ask this question of your statement: Who/What does (or did) what? That simple question will unlock a wordy sentence.

The view from his office window did not please Professor Tobias Mann, who could see little in the cold, fading day but his face's own bright reflection, seemingly bulbous and void of features. The window was too tall and too narrow, giving the impression of a prison. *As though I'm stuck in the gulag,* thought the Humanities Department Chair, feeling alone and more than a little righteous about it. *Why am I here? I'm supposed to be on Thanksgiving break.* Mann imagined all his so-called colleagues warm and cozy—*fat and stupid*—in their homes, splayed out on their couches and eating thick turkey sandwiches, *no doubt,* the Thanksgiving carcasses all picked clean after the endless games of football. Professor Mann did not understand the joy of the gridiron or even the camaraderie of other humans, for that matter, unless he were holding court about his many opinions, which were of course facts. He would not have minded having an ear or two to bend right now, but at present he toiled in anonymity, the only one doing his job at the end of a holiday weekend. Looking down upon the darkening campus, he again saw only his fat face surrounded by the glare of the overhead light. *I don't look human*, he thought, pressing his forehead against the cold glass to see the still quad. *Frost already!* Dark and cold and not a sound to be heard. *Just like winter!* The immense emptiness of the building and the campus and the whole world pushed down on the alienated professor, but he, with a pinch of effort, ignored it. Turning back to the computer screen but still stuck in his own controlled gloom, he didn't really see the spreadsheet, the schedule of courses for the spring semester, half filled out (all the full-timers and half a dozen adjuncts), half to go, the rest of the part-timers. Scheduling was Mann's least favorite responsibility, less because his decisions affected adjunct faculty lives so financially, more because the activity was just so tedious.

Out of the internal gloom loomed a bearded face: Jacobs! *That idiot, that right-wing moron! Bill Jacobs has to go, at last, after all these years. Have to fire the bastard, not schedule him again, not Jacobs!* How many of Jacob's students had filed into this office to complain? His Republican rants in class. What do students care about Republicans? *He's a scary bastard*, he scared the students. The ones who complained were the brave ones, or maybe just angry about their poor grades. Even worse, Jacobs failed too many students, and even worse than that—much worse, since failing could be argued as a sign of high standards, and those were good, those could be waved about to administrators, like that bastard Johns. No, what was worse by far was that Jacobs' students dropped his courses, withdrew after two weeks, or less, and that meant money. That meant grumbling administrators, like that bastard Omar Johns. *Jacobs!*

From this mental fit, Tobias Mann looked placidly at the screen, at the blank spots in the spreadsheet for 8 and 9 a.m., M/W/F, ENG101, sections 14 and 15. At least Bill wanted morning classes, and he was gone by 10:30, 11:00 at the latest. And he was a scary son-of-a-bitch, that's for sure. *Wasn't he in Iraq? Viet Nam?* Old son-of-a-bitch, but probably had guns and bayonets. Could probably kill just with his hands.

Tobias Mann typed "Jacobs" into the two blank ENG101 slots, and then his gaze drifted to sections 1, 2, 6, and 7, M/W/F ENG101 and ENG102, 11 and 12, 3 and 4—all filled in already: Diggerson, Matthew. *Digger. Why do I always start this scheduling with Digger?* He was not that much of an old-timer, and a bit of a bastard, too, smug, seemed a little too confident. *But he was one of us,* he was full-time faculty. The students liked him, too, and didn't withdraw from his classes. *How many of my students withdraw?* They liked Digger better, *that wife loser!* But he was dependable, good for the school, good for the administrators, *good for me.* And he was less insufferable than before his wife left him. *My wife hasn't left me! Amy!* She had hardly said a word at Sunday dinner (meatloaf, thank God—not turkey leftovers), didn't try to stop him when he mentioned going into work to finish scheduling—"to escape all the distractions," he had said, sarcastically, but Amy didn't seem to catch on. Not a great sense of humor. *But at least Amy hasn't left me like Digger's wife did. What was her name? Good looking girl.* Two weeks prior, he had typed "Diggerson" into the spreadsheet, four times, and then finished the full-timers, repeating their preferred schedules and courses. The part-timers would have to wait, take the leavings. Decades back, Professor Mann had been an adjunct faculty member for a handful of semesters, but those few years had been put away, shut in a drawer, locked. Now part-timers were to be looked down upon, to use when needed, to contact with a smile when emergencies arose.

From beyond the frosted window, something from the night ripped at the air, a squawk of some kind, so Tobias Mann searched out into the thin darkness again. *Can't see much except my big white face. Is that frost?* Must have been a gull, sleeping on the roof. Thinking of seagulls having nightmares, the educator smiled, or twisted his lips anyway. Back at the screen, the blank slots for sections 16 and 17 beckoned. Mann tapped the minimize tab and looked at the fall semester, sections 16 and 17, yet his mind immediately drifted again, turned inward, into the twisting, wrestling winds. *That damn student, what's his name, George something?* Who names their kid George nowadays? It was all Connor and Katelyn and Michael and Justin. *George?* That was probably why he was such a donkey in class, such a knucklehead. Did nothing but check his cell phone, didn't even hide it in his lap like the other knuckleheads, either. Right on the desk. Didn't talk to his peers, didn't talk in class, said almost nothing when called upon. Didn't even make some half-assed excuse as to why he wasn't listening. Couldn't be shamed. Missed classes, too, and no excuses there, either. Used to be dead uncles, whole generations of fifty-something men wiped out. Now, it was family emergencies: *I had a "family emergency" and couldn't come to class.* Students were like superheroes, swooping into their family emergencies, which were always past tense, always seemingly solved by a single absence, as though the potential tragedy needed just the student's touch, an eighteen-year-old's, and just a little time, *my class time*, and then all was well. Family emergency averted; *family emergency, my ass!* These students, they deserved Jacobs.

The window bleated again, some muffled night groan, but turning toward the darkness, Mann failed to see beyond his own glowing face, white and puffy, twisted and monstrous. *Well, that's how I feel.* He leaned his monster face closer to the window, and the quad materialized slowly beneath the darkness. *Good old OVC*, he started to rant sarcastically, but then his thoughts softened because the grounds did look pretty and peaceful, empty, student-less, the library with its twin soaring brick towers, the administration building with its wooden historic look, its wrap-around porch, the pathways' periodic lampposts with their softly glowing skirts (Amy would call the color eggshell, no doubt), the empty stages beneath. *What the!* For a moment, the lonely professor saw a shape, a person, caught beneath the lamp outside the Faculty Offices Building, looking up, looking at him. A hooded grayness. Then gone. Just his imagination and the late-November frost. No students stalked the soft lights below. *Now I'm seeing things.* The Chairman glanced at this watch, noted the time. *Past 7, so the kiddies have all eaten, returned to their rooms.* Then Mann remembered that it was still officially Thanksgiving break, that nearly all the students were still off campus or just returning from distant states to their dorms, where they would stay, all filled up with home-cooked food. Or not returned yet at all, not until Monday. Did he take extra days off when he was a student? Tobias could not remember being a student. The returned ones weren't working in their rooms, he decided, more likely planning alcohol acquisition or rolling some doobies, *the little bastards.* The campus appeared definitely empty around the quad, anyway, and that fact made the solitary man feel sadder for himself, for his self-less toiling, his never-ending work, all alone.

He alone amongst the whole world toiled within this dark, soft, cold night, *rent by the nightmares of gulls and stalked by hooded ghosts*, yet how could he finish this scheduling? Too many nagging anxieties, nasty little spirits whacking away with big pick axes. *Whack, whack.* One spirit nagged at him about the scheduling, opined that the chair should have finished it before Thanksgiving, that the part-timers, especially, got nervous about spring scheduling, about not getting enough work. *Pigeons*—they should be glad of the bread tossed in their path, and he imagined the adjunct faculty flapping about him, all squawking at once, and then he conjured up a nice shotgun. Yes, he needed to do some faculty reviewing, some culling, to weed out some of the nuts, especially the ones with complaints against them, with too many early withdrawals. Thinking of the number of *W*'s from his own classes, Tobias Mann shook that thought away and looked at the screen again, at sections 16 and 17: Smith. *I'll give Smith the same schedule.* Paul caused no real problems and had been at the school forever. And the students didn't complain about him, not much, anyway.

But what was that old complaint? Was it about Smith? Why had he considered getting rid of Smith, giving him no courses? Omar Johns, *that bastard*, he told me about it, threw it right in my face after that division meeting. *That administrative sonofabitch, never even taught once, had no idea, no skills for it, and he tossed Smith in my face.* "One of yours," he'd said, and then what? One of yours … something about corporal punishment. One of yours had been resorting to corporal punishment? "Resorting" and "corporal punishment": that was what that bastard said, and he had been serious, hadn't even been smiling. That meeting had been a bitch, long and boring, full of administrators sounding off, blaming faculty for this and that, Johns himself lamenting retention rates and student evaluations, and then that confrontation about Smith. At first, he'd had to think about corporeal punishment's definition, the first image being an execution, a hanging. But then he imagined knuckles being rapped by a ruler, by a nun, who became Jacobs, that bastard, and then, more murkily, Paul Smith, whom he'd never pictured as a knuckle rapper—too old and weak. More like a vulture. Then he'd stood before Omar Johns, open-mouthed, one emotion rising from the ashes of its predecessor: confusion, defensiveness, embarrassment, anger.

"Who's been rapping knuckles with rulers?" he'd said into the administrator's face, and Tobias Mann thought good-naturedly of that question now, *a fine response*. Johns had been open-mouthed after that one. *Johns! Paul's fine; let him rap a knuckle or two.* He clicked the maximize tab, returned to the spring spreadsheet, and typed "Smith" into those two sections. As the minutes passed, the Humanities Chairperson filled in more empty spring slots, noting the part-timers' requests and responsibilities at other schools, scoffing at some of the information, sniffing to release a little pathos, for himself. *Bonner*, he thought at one point, searching for the adjunct's face, muddling the pathos: she was good looking. Dark and vibrant. Could still be a student. Not very friendly, though, cold even. Just wanted her courses. *Thank you and good bye.* "Well, we will see, Elena," Tobias Mann said quietly to the empty office. "We will see."

Apparently, he did "see," for Mann typed "Bonner" into one cell, then another, then looked back to the fall schedule to find other names, clicking back and forth from past to future, the spring semester. *Drudgery*, he concluded, and after each added name, Mann paused to form criticisms and to look out the dark window inscribed with his grotesquely lit features. *My better half*, Professor Tobias Mann laughed to himself, feeling less alone, less insignificant.

The hooded figure entered the unlocked Faculty Offices Building carefully, quietly, at around 8:30 p.m., and as soon as the door hissed shut, the newcomer squeezed in the building's warmth, its welcome. A nice feeling: *I'm home!* From the cold outside, the entire building was dark except for one window, *his* window. A big dead building. Four stories of darkness with just one flicker of life, Mann's window at the far left, third floor. The newcomer had been in that office before, *oh, many times!* Had never gotten a wisp of satisfaction from those visits, either, just the relief of leaving that room. Passive in Mann's office, weak, just an object each time, *but tonight would be different!* The doer would be *done*, object becoming the subject—action itself. The hero in this little drama called life. *Just like the forefathers!* At that thought, the shrouded figure smiled, but no face could be seen, just the gleam of eyes, maybe teeth, inside the folded grey hood. The hood moved into the building.

Up the stairs, through the dark, step by step, seeing by the dim safety light in the middle of each stairwell. Up the steps, turn, turn, up the steps to the third floor. The figure looked half like a human, half like a grim reaper minus the scythe and black shroud—a modern reaper in sweats. As the being passed from stairwell to waiting area, the landing door exuded a little hiss, too, air escaping maybe, but Mann's office was too far away for worries. *No fear!* The hooded presence smiled again to release the hounds, shaking the hood, too, feeling the prickling anxiety click apart from neck and shoulders, breaking the thin *chicken* bones, squashing any last doubts. *I am the stalker here, the wolf. The Wolf will use the shadows to reach the prey.* When pitted against the wild, civilization really had no chance.

Through the third-floor door, two choices unfolded: right into darkness, left into shadows with a slash of light. Far away light. Then the silence snapped beneath a sharp sound—a cry, a howl? *No.* Just the wind, or maybe a gull, the muffled scream and yodel of a seagull—EEEaahyut, yut, yut!— waking up within the blackness, struggling from a dream of killing or being killed. The noise had momentarily rattled the intruder, but the sound came from the wild, from a kindred darkness. With that buoying image, the Wolf focused on breathing, closed its eyes, raised an upper lip, waited for the heart to slow, waited for the predator's heart—*steady, ready.* To the left, the slash of light gave the darkness length and purpose.

The ghostly human figure moved slowly down the left corridor, a shadow within the shadows. In the mind, the hallway could be stood on end and imagined as a deep hole, the lighted opening beckoning the other upward. *Yes, must climb out of this deep place, pull up from rung to rung, toward the waiting light.* Adrenaline shivered up the body and drifted toward the light like some night insects. *Mann deserves to die!* How many peers would agree! No one would admit to it, but they all hated Tobias Mann, and they would all be thankful, beneath their breaths, out of the hearing of the rest. *The rest!* Mann was enough for this night.

The hooded Wolf closed out the darkness, let it trail away. The corridor righted itself, and Mann's office light spilled out like a tongue into the hallway and gave the approaching creeping figure legs, a torso, arms, and then a sliver of face, a fixed smile, dry and shallow behind the grey veil. In the right hand, silver and pointed, death itself glittered, having emerged from the front pocket of the hooded sweatshirt. Two doors down from the source of light, the stalker stopped. *To do this is to leave life, to cross society's thickest shield.* The creeper's head felt light, as though it could detach itself and float away, up out of this semi-dark tunnel, up through the ceiling. Legs felt heavy now, too, each step pronounced, considered, and beneath the mask, both lips had turned down, lost their fire. The Wolf's heart beat too fast. Sounds no longer entered ears, but exited the suddenly still form instead. Blood pounded, adrenaline crackled, breaths wheezed and drifted toward the light. Then the silver knife made its weight known, and as it was raised up in two hands, the terrible steel glinted, ignited. Within the hood, the intruder gazed at the gleaming offering and thought of those who had in the past wielded the knife, former wolves who did the job, who did what must be done, took care of history's enemies. *Emotions must be controlled! Blood steadied. Action taken.*

Feet shuffled forward carefully. Ten feet from the door, mere steps from the goal, the light began to cling and tried to mock, illuminating reality, highlighting passivity and place. Too far advanced now, the Wolf heard mouse sounds and then recognized key strokes: Tap, tap, tap. Tap, tap, tap. Little mouse tappings. *Poor little mouse!* Advancing toward the taps, scuttling with the key strokes, peeking inside—the scene laid out exactly as imagined: Mann faced away from the door, focusing on the screen, paying no attention to anyone but himself, *as always.*

The Wolf let the silver blade lead, the great canine fang, serrated and thirsty, and from the dark edges of the window a whiteness grew in the top-left corner. Frost framed the ghostly shapes, the big one and the other, the expanding one, and the hooded presence could hear the wind now, moaning, scrabbling at the pane to be let inside.

Chapter Two: Subordination

> *If you make too many statements, your readers will not see how all those points relate, so everything will have the same level of importance—just a list of thoughts. Thus arises the need for subordination, for "although" and "if," for "because," "when," and "since." For any idea to stand out in importance, one or more others must slide back, must be subordinate.*

When the phone rang, Digger thought immediately of his mother and then of his head, which seemed to be swelling and pulsating. *Oh, God! Why do I do it? Why don't I stop after two beers or four? On a school night, no less!* Then the phone bonged again, more like a shriek actually, and more thoughts leaked out of Matthew Diggerson's consciousness: What did his mother want? Where was Simba? She needed to go out, he needed to go out, then to school, and coffee, *I need coffee!* The phone blared again, then again.

"Hello," he said, a little harsher than he meant to, but his head throbbed.

"What's the matter?" his mother asked. "You sound unhappy. Have you been thinking of Anna?"

Just every day for more than seven years! What else was there to think about? So, no, he told his mother he had not been thinking about his ex-wife, had not talked to her in years, and that she knew that. "I'm getting ready for school," he added, a little softer but firmer. "I have class at eleven." The pains in his head seemed to want release through his eye holes. When he took his palms from his squinting eyes, Digger discovered two deep brown globes streaked with golden light gazing up at him with concern. Simba shuffled her front legs up and down, a habit that usually foreshadowed conversation. "Woof" she whispered, blinking, pointy ears shifting like little satellite dishes. All at once, Digger's head hurt less, a little. Holding the phone away from his head, Digger repeated that he had to go to school.

The voice on the phone ignored Digger's work facts, well-known words picking up steam: that she was doing as well as could be expected for a seventy-three-year-old woman, that life was not the same anymore, blah, blah. He cut in to say that she was doing very well from what he could see, that seventy was no longer old, and that he could not talk now, that Simba needed to go out. The woman who brought him into this world ignored his dog, too, and started in on his Uncle John, the "damn fool," and his refusal to get a hearing aid, and then on to his two aunts, both older than his mother, who refused to give up their driver's licenses. "They're going to kill themselves," she informed Digger, "or somebody else, some innocent bystander." Digger had heard this news many times. His family, what was left of them, all sang the same songs, the same dirges. Digger said that Carol and Mary needed their mobility and independence, but those two points sailed by, found no docking harbor. Digger glanced down at his grinning dog, who no doubt did need to pee. Digger needed to pee, too. Then his mother said, "You know, as you get older, the world gets younger." She added that Digger would not understand that "for a little while." Digger responded that he "didn't understand much now, that's for sure," and then said that he would call his mother later, that Simba absolutely had to go out. He thought of asking his mother why she had called, but didn't, worried about a fresh torrent of words. Goodbyes traveled the lines, but just prior, his mother punctuated the call with "You're not getting any younger either, Matthew, you know!" And then she added, "And your school is cancelled today," and hung up.

Digger breathed hard into the sweet silence, for he had been holding his breath. Then the disheveled, middle-aged man (yes, early forties was middle age, another lurch in the hand of time) thought "cancelled," and looked down at Simba. Since that simple movement ignited shiny ribbons that gleamed and nagged at his eyes, Matthew Diggerson pressed fingers into both sides of his head, his temples, closing his eyes again, and felt turbulence, the moving earth. *My mother tells me that school is cancelled?* Had he reverted back in time? He did not feel old, not usually, but since reaching thirty-five a handful of years past, he now could acknowledge time, its presence and flow, especially since he'd met that milestone alone—with neither his wife nor his dog. His dog—when he connected orbs with the short, big-headed dog, the man shed years. Maybe that was what his mother meant, that he and other middle-agers looked younger now that his mother had started sliding through the seventies.

Who knows? Simba continued to sit and look up at him, concerned by the deep sigh. "I'm fine and how are you?" said Digger, scuffling the tan hound's head, bending over to do so since Simba had oddly short legs, the offspring of a corgi and something bigger, some short-haired hound. Although bending did nothing to improve the demolition work taking place in his cranium, Digger petted his dog for half a minute or so, Simba's grin widening around her black muzzle, her dark, pointy ears rotating, and then she followed him into the kitchen, where Digger poured a cup of yesterday's coffee into a mug, stuck it into the microwave, selected one minute, pondered about OVC, and then let Simba out the back door, glancing at the bright day and then grimacing. He strode into the little bathroom off the kitchen and wondered again what his mother meant about the world's getting younger. His mother didn't often tell him something unexpected. She must have had it backwards, he decided; she must have meant "older." She and her peers were all aging, as were neighbors, Digger himself. He made a point to ask her about it, returning to the kitchen to look out the window for Simba, who was nosing beneath the spindly blue spruce, motionless (no wind today), and then at the microwave clock: just five more seconds. When the appliance dinged, Digger felt better already, and he sipped the coffee as he called Simba back in (not too cold out today) and then returned to the living room. *Cancelled?* Digger slumped down at his desk, then clicked on the computer to check email. Simba flopped behind the chair, joining in as usual, guarding the silent house against noisy intrusion. The man sipped more coffee, deleted emails, slurped coffee.

From the list of a dozen black unread emails, Digger saw one from Ocean View, an "emergency" message, the type sent to announce snow cancellations. *I'll be damned*, he thought. His mother had been right, *as usual*. "Classes cancelled, November 26, Monday." No explanation, just an extension of Thanksgiving break. Digger experienced a little wave of happiness run up into his head, a little glow of freedom, but it glimmered away and left a muffled throbbing, attenuating. He'd never seen an email like this. *Could it be a fake?* Most of the pains in his head had receded, forgotten.

Digger got up and went back to the phone, one of two landlines in the house, for the writing professor refused to get a cell phone, didn't want to be reached at any moment. Anna had owned the cell, so Digger had thought he was safe in case of car trouble, the only reason he could think of for owning a cell phone. In Digger's wake, Simba trailed along and then flumped over, laying herself down in one smooth motion, butt first, then long body, and finally her big head. Simba looked a bit like a short-legged, lightly furred German shepherd with more of a boxy face, the head of a paperless hound, a mutt. This oddity was accented by a mound of hair just behind her head, basically a mane, like a lion's. The image of beauty, the dog of many breeds glanced repeatedly up at Digger, a human of many breeds himself, and Simba looked a little sad the way dogs do at rest. One pointy ear stuck almost straight up, a common sight when Simba slept. Seeing that furry triangle, Digger always imagined a sail, pictured Simba journeying away into dreamland. *Take me*, he had thought at these times.

His hangover just a mist now, just translucent vapors, Digger called the school but got only an automated message: classes cancelled, no staff at all required, not until Tuesday— or "until further notice." *That's very strange*—never happened. Even on snow days, much of the staff had to show up. Digger leaned down to pat Simba's head, which immediately rose up in attention. "No school!" he said, and the dog's mouth broke open in a long, wide grin. Usually, Digger felt a blush of excitement on snow days, yet that feeling was muted now. He had had a nice active lesson plan for today, one that would have gotten students moving around, but he could move it to Wednesday. He got his briefcase, sat back at his desk, and checked Wednesday's plan, crossing out a revision exercise that involved sticking to the assignment's purpose. Then he heated up another cup of coffee and returned to his desk and revised lesson, his mind adrift. The house was completely quiet, not even muffled wind sounds or seagulls yelling. Living on the ocean, Digger always heard the wind, pulling the waves forward and yanking at the spindly blue spruce he had planted in his little back yard, yet today the ocean held its breath.

Must be some accident at Ocean View, Digger concluded— *maybe pipes*. But it was not cold enough yet for that, a little frost maybe, a hint of winter, but not the bone-chilling temperature plunge that froze and burst pipes. *Wind, then*, for last night the winds had really howled. The winds must have ripped off some roofing, making the campus a danger, keeping everyone away. Digger walked from the living room to the kitchen and looked out the back door at the circular thermometer, showing two cardinals, one red and one green, a couple stuck happily in time. That was what he had wanted to be. The thermometer's arrow pointed to low forties. His spruce still stood motionless in the left corner of his little backyard, like a photograph, time stopped. Then a real cardinal, blood red, broke the vision by landing on one of the thin green branches, and Digger watched it leap around, searching for danger, then grabbing a seed and taking off inland. He knew that the male's dark-green mate would be nearby. He was probably bringing the seed to her. Digger rested his head against the glass and stared left as far as possible, seeing his little black pickup truck but no cardinals, male or female. Then he shifted his other temple against the cold glass and looked to the right. The ocean—the upper throat of the bay, actually—showed shy wisps of whitecaps, fewer than usual, and Digger heard only the silence of his beautiful, lonely home.

Peeling himself from the cool caress of the glass, he retreated to his living room, to his computer (Simba trailing behind for she had followed him into the kitchen, as always), and considered emailing Elena Bonner, another writing teacher at Ocean View College, asking if she knew what was up. She wouldn't, though, she was just part-time, but Digger liked her better than any of his other colleagues, full or part time. He had even considered asking her out, had been contemplating doing so for three years at least, since the moment she'd arrived at OVC. An adjunct, she was not in the loop, though. She might even have been at the community college now, unless that were closed, too. What was her schedule this semester? What was her cell number? Digger didn't know, and that fact made him feel a little guilty. Why did he push life away, except for the birds out his window, the spruce tree, except for Simba? *Enough of guilt!* Not even supplied by his mother this time.

Life is guilt, Digger decided, switching his thoughts to Ocean View College's full-time composition professors. Which full-timer might know what was happening? Tobias, if anyone, but Digger rarely emailed Tobias Mann. He was no friend, truth be told. Did Digger even have friends anymore? Anna had always had the friends, had always made the social engagements, which had dried up over the years. Who wanted a third wheel? *Broken spokes.* Digger looked over at Simba, who returned the greeting, head down again but always alert, her big eyes shifting. *Maybe Don would know something.* Don Domberg at Tutorial Services—he knew everyone and everything at OVC. A decade ago, when Digger had been just part-time, he had made extra money tutoring for Don, but when Digger was hired full-time, he quit that side job, didn't need the money and wanted more time at home with Anna. *Anna, what had she wanted?* She had said that she wanted to travel, wanted to see a bigger world than Ocean View, but Digger never believed her. Anna just wanted a different man, that was what he believed, someone who didn't live with words but with actions. From Anna, always from Anna, Digger drifted back to tutoring, to the one-on-one work helping other people's students, the camaraderie and purity of the teaching. Maybe he should talk to Don Domberg about tutoring again; maybe he could bring Simba to Tutorial Services. Turning to the computer, Digger emailed Don about the school cancellation (not about tutoring, not yet) and then headed back to the coffee pot, back to the door leading to his little lawn and then to the big ocean. His spruce still stood rigid, motionless, not even a quiver. No bird movement enlivened the portrait of a lonely man's view.

How often had he stood at this back door and watched this wondrous postcard of the world, this art come to life? As usual, Digger cast his glance far and wide, out above the horizon on the distant shore, then at the shore itself (bigger houses and back lawns, greener with outside stone barbecues), then to the sea, just undulating greyly beneath the cool blue November sky, sleeping almost, to his own shore (thirty yards of sand and then ten more of tall tan sea grass, like swords buried hilt down), to his picket fencing (green, not white), his little patch of grass (some grass anyway), his spruce, the pole with the feeder, where two chickadees were now playing get-the-seed, one at a time, flitting from feeder to spruce branch, repeatedly. Digger watched them, imagining that he could hear their distinct, happy self-referencing call, but the scene was silent, just the tinny white sound of the turning earth, a shifting beyond human hearing or perhaps embedded deep within it. Digger's mind returned to the cancellation. Although the scene beyond his gaze represented the picture of harmony, he felt uneasy, troubled. He had never liked change, and this blue, somewhat motionless morning hid something darker, more turbulent. Maybe, though, his mother's call had simply unsettled him, her mention of Anna, of his deaf uncle, of his aging aunts—all their refusals and the oncoming wave of youth.

Simba appeared to his right, to the spot where the door would open, *smart girl*, and looked up at him, woofing once, a grunting sound that was almost a bark, almost a word. With her long tan body and neck ruff, her triangle ears and black muzzle, she had reminded Digger immediately of a female lion, and five years ago, a handful of years after he had been elevated to full-time status, two years after Anna had left (to find herself, to lose him), he had brought her home from the pound. They had saved each other and still did, every day.

"Simba, do you want to go for a walk?" Digger watched the long body start to wave, back end first, the tail leading the charge, and he almost reached for the leash but instead glanced back out the door, thinking of façades and of his diminished energy level, only half seeing the pretty scene. Past his little backyard was a homemade gate (Digger had made it himself, out of wood, wire, and screws) and then a narrow path through the pointy sea grass, thigh high. Digger had heard somewhere that it was illegal to cut the sea grass, to damage it in any way, but he had pulled some out so that he could pass to the beach without rowing through the tall grass, imagining each jabbing frond to be ridden by a tick, a little Lyme-disease carrying horror, ready to wipe itself onto Simba, onto his pant legs, to start sucking and transmitting misery. To be sure, Digger had a phobia about that grass, but only since getting Simba. Back when Anna had lived in the little house, for two years before she had left it and him, Digger would take walks alone sometimes, and when he entered the back door would yell, "Honey, I'm home!" mimicking a movie. But he had not hollered those words for close to eight years. In the seven years, three months AA (After Anna), he had come through that back door thousands of times, never once announcing himself, never feeling a welcoming warmth, except for Simba's, the pup glad to be home in the cold harbor.

I have become a subordinate clause, Matthew Diggerson realized—a group of words waiting for a statement, waiting to be made whole. *Pathetic*, he concluded, and he was reaching for Simba's leash when the phone rang, jarring him. Immediately he thought of his mother again, for rarely did he hear another voice on the end of the landline. Sometimes telemarketers would call wanting to know his advice—*why?* He was hardly a consumer. He was hardly part of society at all. If he had lived with a handful of cats instead of one sweet dog, neighbors would have forgotten his name and referred to him with jibes and whispers as the Crazy Cat Man. The phone called again, demanding, sounding harsh in the silence with the sun slanting in, and Digger felt a trickle of irrational fear. The phone blared again. Stupid, he told himself and snatched it up, prepared for his mother, but it was not a seventy-three year old woman this time.

"Professor Diggerson, Matthew Diggerson," said a man with the tone of a statement more than a question.

Digger responded that it was, hesitant, about to add "Who's this?" when the voice started again: "This is Detective Doyle from the OVPD. Are you aware of an incident at the college last night?"

A question that sounds like an accusation—Digger thought of his mother and said hesitantly, "I know that classes are cancelled today. I've emailed colleagues about it. Did you say 'incident'? What kind of incident?"

The policeman ignored Digger, said instead that they needed to talk, that he needed to talk with all faculty, that

Digger's name had come up first, and that Digger had to come to the station, right now, "if that is convenient."

This guy uses no subordination, thought Digger. He talked with a string of statements, like my mother, and why did his name "come up"? Why "first?" His last name started with "D," but what about Elena? Hers started with "B." But she was part-time, of course, and this cop must be looking at the full-time faculty. Then Digger recognized the long pause, experienced a little guilt, a dab of fear, uncertainty.

"Why did my name come up?"

"We need to talk with all faculty members. We can talk at the station," said Doyle, and Digger thought again, *it's like talking to my mother*.

"Did somebody get hurt?"

"At the station," said Doyle. "Can you come over right now?"

Chapter Three: Semicolons

*If you ask a student what punctuation mark should be added to a
model sentence, he or she will inevitably say incorrectly,
"Semicolon." Because semicolons function basically like a period,
more often than not, they are misused since they should be commas,
sometimes colons. A correct semicolon should balance two related
full thoughts, often replacing "and" or "but" phrasing—like a soft
period. If you add one to a sentence, check both sides of the mark:
do you make two equally important statements?*

Digger left Simba at home, didn't want to lock her in the
cab of his little Toyota pickup, unable to picture strolling into
the police station with a dog. Summoned to the police station.
Digger held that thought at bay by concentrating on the traffic
and squinting against the sun's glare. From the radio, he
received no news about OVC, just about a house fire and then
some political scandal. The world outside his truck appeared
so sunny and normal, yet on the mile or so drive (everything
in Ocean View was "a mile or so"), he could not completely
block out that old DWI (were they now called DUI?), knew
that the detective would see it in Digger's file (his "record"),
and fretted about it. *Nobody got hurt; nobody died—except his
old pickup truck.* He had loved that truck, and his new one
was not the same even though it had grown on him these past
seven years. In the old truck, Anna had existed: her imprint
on the passenger seat, her aura. The post-Anna truck carried
neither cell nor scent of her, and that fact always bothered
Digger as he drove about. Now, though, he worried about the
DWI and the police, especially about Detective Doyle.
    In the station's parking lot, he worried also about where to
park—seemed to be cop cars all over the place—so he drove

to the back row and pulled in next to a marked SUV. When he got out, a gull veered overhead and screamed, sounding like a slaughtered pig drifting into a giant reptilian gurgle—EEEEaaYut, yut, yut, yut, yut—and Digger froze, said "Jesus!" aloud, and then imagined the response of OVC's janitor, the religious maintenance man. *Dost thou not use the Lord's name in vain!* Something like that. Digger noted that the wind had picked up, streaming between the two vehicles, making the moment feel more threatening and symbolic, but at least clearing Digger's mind of the morning's muddle. Washed out by sky scream and the invisible winds, he felt empty now, but on guard, as though he were going to the dentist or to the doctor to hear about cavities, blood test results, cholesterol levels.

At the front desk, Digger encountered a jowly, silent police officer, an Officer Martin if the desk plaque could be trusted. "Can I help you?" the cop said with no accent on the "help" and without introducing himself.

"Officer Doyle, Detective, is expecting me."

"OVC," replied the jowled cop knowingly. "Officer Doyle, Detective, is down the corridor," and the unfriendly man nodded his head to the right, as though conserving energy. Ignoring the surly cop, already looking past him to the telephone one with all the questions, Digger said "thank you," and feeling like a high school student sent to the principal, he moved on down the short hallway, only six doors, three on each side. The first one on the left announced "Detective John Doyle," a gold-plated plaque that looked like metal, not the plastic one on Digger's own office door, his name typed and slipped into the plastic—*easy in, easy out* (or would be, if not for tenure). Realizing the rattle and pop of raw nerves, Digger shook his arms a bit, stretched his neck to either side, and knocked on the door—three good raps, solid.

A man's voice came clearly though the door: "Yes." Digger pulled the door open and found a small office with a big desk and a Doyle he didn't expect. The detective looked short (a squat torso), but not fat, and boasted sandy hair neither long nor short—not the buzz-cut Digger was expecting. Doyle's somewhat length-deprived arms both rested on his desktop, parallel, as though he were about to be handed a child, and Digger thought irrationally of the baby Jesus. Then he realized that this cop looked sort of like him, like Digger, not like Jesus—just a little shorter, both body and hair. *About my age, too.* The comparisons lightened Digger's mood a bit, took the edge off a few nerves.

"Professor Diggerson," announced the little detective, just a hint of a question, a slight rise on the "son," and then the policeman motioned Digger into the one available chair before the desk. And frowned—*was that a frown?*

"Yes," said Digger, adding "Detective Doyle," and he leaned forward in the chair, as though ready to leap up at the sound of a starting pistol or perhaps to clang together two frosty mugs in a toast to each other's health. Digger's mind often focused on strange comparisons, which had always amused Anna. But analogies were not enough to support a union, to carry a life. Digger waited for the policeman to start. More nervous than curious, the teacher, by nature somewhat quiet, felt words pushing around his brain. They wanted out, and the motionless cop did not help matters. Finally, Digger gave in to temptation: "What's this all about? I heard no news on the radio, but you mentioned an 'incident' at Ocean View. My own mother called to tell me that school was cancelled. Was there some sort of attack, or some accident? Is everyone all right? I'm very concerned and can get nobody to answer my emails. Can you tell me what happened and why you want to talk to faculty members? Are the students okay?"

Digger shut up, tap off, and felt a little foolish, as Doyle sat back and watched him stammer about with the questions. *Probably what guilty people do*, thought Digger, determined not to be intimidated, to parallel the other man's ease and innocence. For what seemed like minutes, the two men gazed at each other in silence. *He looks like me with a purpose*, Digger concluded.

"Professor Diggerson, due to last night's incident at the college, I need to ask some questions, just routine, big-picture enquiries. I need to understand the background."

After these perplexing announcements, Doyle shifted forward in his chair (were they about to toast?), and the interrogation began: He was Professor Matthew Diggerson? *He is*. He was forty-one years old? *Yes, old and getting older*. He had been teaching at Ocean View College for several years? *Fifteen years or so*. He was full time? *For about ten years*. He was divorced? *Seven years, three months, six days*. He lived at 111 Cottage View? *For about ten years*. He had one DUI? *Yes, an old one, seven years old, but none since*. Digger sputtered on a bit about the DUI, one of the bigger mistakes of his life, he said, as his old pickup truck could attest to. The cop offered no judgments, though, and just let him talk. Making his fumbling excuses, Digger suddenly felt like a criminal, like prey. Did the cops know that he still got blindingly drunk? Could they somehow monitor his beer intake, find out how much he bought, check his recyclables? *Why not?* Digger determined, but that would just show them that he did not drink too much (at least too often) since he didn't. He went days, even weeks, without drinking. His recyclable bin carried no more than the average man's, probably far less. Once he started, though, . . . and Digger stopped his mind from finishing that thought.

However, Doyle chose not to linger on Digger's past problem with drinking and driving. His hands on the keyboard, his eyes on Digger, the detective switched topics but continued his interrogatory barrage. He was a colleague of Professor Tobias Mann? *Yes*. Mann was the Department Chairperson? *Yes*. Mann had had that title for three years? *About that*. Would he, Digger, like to be Department Chairperson? *No, too much paperwork and meetings*. Would any of his colleagues have those aspirations? *Maybe, probably, but none had ever mentioned it to him, not that he could remember.* Did any of his colleagues have problems with Professor Mann? *No major problems that he could think of.* How about minor problems? *Well, there were always scheduling conflicts and department objectives, but nothing worth killing over, and any other chair would bring those same problems.* Why did you mention 'killing'? *A term of speech.* Was the professor well-liked by his colleagues? *Respected, well-liked enough. They all get along, anyway.* By his students? Digger paused because a thought would not form; then another did. Digger cut into the questions.

"Is Tobias all right? Why are you asking all these questions about Tobias?"

Doyle had been taking notes, typing Digger's responses into his PC after asking the questions and watching Digger's immediate reactions, making Digger feel a little guilty and a little angry, too. Shifting just his dark eyes, not his head, Doyle looked at Digger, as though analyzing his two questions, and Digger realized that Doyle looked more like an accountant than a cop, although he had no accountant friends and didn't know if he had ever actually even seen an accountant. The cop didn't really look like Digger. *Too stiff.* Doyle didn't move his head enough. *Even my mind is blathering on*, Digger thought, creating related thoughts, one linked precariously to the next.

"Professor Mann was killed last night," said Doyle, finally, his eyes on Digger. "He was found deceased in his office. His body was found this morning, at 8:37, by a Jessica Williams, who is your department's secretary, if I have that right."

Digger said that he did have that right because Jess Williams was in fact their secretary, and his mind just floated away because he could not get his head around the other thing, the "killing" of Tobias. His face scrunched, Digger found himself staring out the window, at some swaying branches, a Maple tree, still some maroon leaves clinging, holding on (how could they still be holding on this late into November?), and then he felt the silence and his own open mouth gaping.

"I find this hard to believe. You say 'killed,' do you mean that Tobias was murdered? Why would anyone kill a teacher? Do you know who did it?" Digger asked the question, not the squat detective, but then he did: "Do you, Professor Diggerson, know who did it?"

Digger had no ideas, but then Bill Jacob's angry face drifted into his thoughts, Bill's inappropriate laughter and conservative bent, his peppered beard and big fingers, and then Mann's sharp, hairless face, his arrogance, his nose in the air, and Digger mentally ticked off colleagues who didn't care for their department head, and he could not think of any who did. Tobias seemed a little rough with the part-timers, especially.

"I have no idea," responded Digger, and Doyle just gave him space to think. "I have no idea. Tobias is, was, not the friendliest person, but nobody I know hated him, not enough to kill him. Who would kill him? Who would murder an English professor? Are you sure it wasn't suicide?"

The little detective chose to hear just the last question. "Why would you think suicide? Was Professor Mann depressed or upset?"

Digger pictured Tobias and then his wife, Amy, her big hair, her arrogance. Digger had a bad opinion of Amy, but maybe that was more his fault, his history, than hers. "No," he said to the policeman. "Tobias did not seem at all suicidal to me. How did he die?"

But that information could not be "divulged" at this point. Facts were still being gathered. The diagnosis was "pending on the final report from the pathologist."

That word, pathologist, seemed too big for Ocean View, so it stuck in Digger's mind. "You have a pathologist?" he asked, but Doyle ignored him. Digger ignored the ignoring because his mind was racing and because faces kept dipping into his consciousness—Tobias,' Amy's, Bill Jacobs,' even Anna's (where had she come from?). Doyle was staring at him again, apparently looking for reactions, and Digger felt blood rushing, could almost hear it. In his mind the faces kept appearing and disappearing, as in one of those Magic 8-Ball toys he had as a kid.

Then Doyle came to some conclusion and continued with his questions—about colleagues, students, the school—typing Digger's short (*and unhelpful*, thought Digger) replies into the appropriate boxes. During these interrogatives, Digger felt a pulse deep within his head and wondered if his breath smelled like alcohol, like stale beer, like scotch, because alcohol breath always reeked like scotch. He sat back a bit, but didn't feel comfortable that way, so he leaned forward again, trying to find some security. Back and forth, the questions, the answers, like a see-saw, and Digger remembered that he had described semicolons that way, as balancers, the middles of see-saws. His mind unorganized, uncontrolled, he realized with relief that the interrogation was just about over (*it must be*) and started to think of his next step: he did not know what that step should be.

"What should I do?" he asked Doyle, feeling like a rudderless teenager, a dingy floating off into a sea with only sky as horizons. Doyle said that the school would be closed for at least two days, that his building was a crime scene, that no one would be allowed into the Faculty Building until at least Wednesday, that he would contact Digger if more answers were needed, that he could go now, that he was "free" to go. *Free?* That bitter word, and Digger's pupils dilated, the sides of his mouth contracting. He wondered if the policeman noticed. Doyle's eyes did not seem to blink, and Digger pictured a cat, a lizard, a corpse—Tobias.

When Digger straightened up, Detective Doyle stayed seated, and Digger concluded that the other man would not rise because he was short, image conscious, human after all. Then Doyle half rose and extended his hand, normal sized and dry: "Thank   you   for   coming   in   so   quickly,   Professor

Diggerson. You were the first faculty member to answer my call. If you see or speak to any of your colleagues, please refer them to me. Do not tell them about Professor Mann. I will be in touch if needed."

Doyle's handshake was quick and confident, a single pump, direct and dismissive—the leading man in this dance, a dance of deception? *Ah*, but Digger noticed that the detective did seem quite short, crouched and leaning forward, now dropping back to his seat, to his work. Digger exited a bit stiffly, thinking of the little detective and of Mann, still stunned by the shocking news, and then he thought of Amy Mann and then of Anna. *At least my wife didn't kill me.* Digger recognized the absurdity of that thought and then shifted his mind to Bill Jacobs, right-wing, argumentative, no doubt a gun owner, no friend of Tobias,' but he chose not tell these thoughts to the policeman. To Detective Doyle, he cast no suspicions at all—except perhaps on himself.

Chapter Four: Mind Mapping

> To delve into potential focusing topics, try using a visual
> element, a mind map, branching one thought off of another,
> repeatedly, to build a tapestry of ideas, a web of interrelated
> thoughts. Better than a simple list, ideas in visual form connect
> causes and effects, stream into examples, link ideas both great and
> small, both broad and specific, and with all of that information, you
> give yourself choices. If you want to create a great college essay, do
> not rush the ideas-generating process.

After leaving the police station, Digger still felt lost, a
combination of shock and relief. Tobias' murder seemed
fictional, yet here Digger was, walking through a police
department parking lot, beneath a coldly glaring sun. He was
relieved to be out of the little detective's glare, or was he?
Digger felt watched—the sun was just so bright—and
directionless. He just could not decide where to go. He walked
slowly to his little pickup and noted the maple tree outside
Doyle's office window, the brave leaves still clinging.
Glancing at the window, Digger saw only empty panes. *The
diminutive Doyle should have one of these little trucks*, he
thought, but then Digger shook his head to release the false
bravado. Tobias had been murdered. School was off until at
least Wednesday, and it was Monday now. Digger thought of
Simba, but then the silence and emptiness of the cottage
pushed that avenue away. He could check email, yet he would
have to go home for that or to the school. *What to do?* The
November sunlight blinded and bothered him, and Digger's
mouth was dry. All at once, he felt the urge for a woman, for
female companionship, and imagined Anna, but she was far
away, years away, gone. He next pictured Elena Bonner; he

could drop by her apartment building, knew vaguely where it was. She could not have killed Tobias, could she? *Why would she?* Because she was tired of toiling as an adjunct, knew that she was a far better teacher than Tobias, wanted to create a full-time opening. *That's insane!* She would not know a thing about the murder, so he could fill her in—but then he remembered that the short policeman, Doyle, asked him to tell no one. He paused outside the black Toyota's door, thinking about his own height, knowing that Anna had wanted a taller man, feeling small, sophomoric.

Once upon a time, he thought, he was not timid; he was happy or at least content. His failed marriage changed him, drawing him inward, away from people. If not for Simba, Digger sometimes imagined that he would fall into himself and disappear. Unsettled, un-tethered, alone in the back of a police parking lot, Digger realized with surprise that Tobias' death had made him want people, that he needed some humanity, so he got into the pickup and went to find some.

Ocean View Coffee was once Karl's Clam Shack, and Digger remembered going there with Anna. Before Karl's, it was something else, a gift shop or used clothes store. Digger often chose the coffee shop because he liked the green interior (paint and spider plants) and because the place reminded him of a past that at times he still romanticized. Plus, the coffee was strong. And in the back booth, he could close his eyes and feel Anna's presence, or at least her ghost. The ghost always ordered a low-fat blueberry muffin, heated, with half a pat of butter.

Also, the workers were friendly but not pushy. They asked how he was doing, obviously recognized him (or at least a tipping customer), but they went no further with questions, other than what he wanted. They left him alone in that corner booth because they somehow knew (at least he imagined that they did) that he was a professor and a writer, always entering with a pen and notebook and retreating with his black coffee and often an old-fashioned donut to the furthest booth, hidden somewhat by the groping tendrils of spider plants. Secluded, Digger knew that he was—or used to be—the subject of conversation, of commiseration, a man abandoned. How did they know that? Did abandonment leave a mark on his face, on his speech, on the way he carried his arms and swung his legs? *The workers all tell themselves that they cannot imagine the feeling of abandonment*, Digger told himself, and he thought, *They will; they will.*

Today, Digger did not think about the workers and their whispered pity, for Tobias' murder grew larger and larger in his thoughts, obliterating tangents. He said hello to the usual girl—Jamie, he remembered seeing on a name tag—and after thanking Jamie, he retreated to his booth with black coffee and a donut. A practitioner of his preaching, Digger took a lot of notes, listing observations about nature and humanity, but mainly about teaching (publish or perish, after all), so now he placed his "food" on the pine table top and opened the notebook toward the middle, where the white-lined pages beckoned. In the middle of one, he wrote "Tobias," and immediately he made a short line to the word "Anger." From there, he added another short line to "Revenge" and a parallel one to "Retribution." *Who, though, and why?* From "Revenge," he penned a blue line to Bill Jacobs, and from that name to three parallel word groups, one right after the other: Slighted? Reprimanded? Schedule problem? From "Reprimanded," he created another line, close to the page's edge now, saying "Student complaint." From there, he snuck in a "Who?" because although most teachers got bitched about every now and again, Digger seemed to remember something serious, just a little different, about a Tobias/student rumor. For now, though, that long line had gone dry. Once every minute or so, Digger sipped the hot coffee and pulled pieces off the plain donut. The clouds in his head from the morning were now long swept away.

Back to the middle of his notes, to Tobias—besides anger, why else would a human murder another? *Envy?* He wrote a line and then "Envy," but he didn't really believe it, and no more lines formed until he thought of Don Domberg. Didn't he once complain about Tobias? The memory eluded Digger, so he slashed one more line from Domberg: Stuck at Tutorial Services?

Leaving envy, he added "Despair," then hesitated before repeating "Jacobs," which led from a short line to "Professional Crossroads?" Could that be it? A man approached the end of middle age, saw the further end but no sweet path to it, rotted inside, lashed out at a convenient target, at the symbol of all gone bad. Digger thought of himself and agreed that the motive could be valid. Who else around Tobias could feel such despair? *Adjuncts?* Adjuncts with their tenuous schedules and shaky futures. But then he focused on another name, making a short line to "Amy," the wife, whom Digger had met on a few occasions only, a couple of times at school functions, once at Tobias' house for a Christmas party. He even dropped an exclamation point after Amy's name. At that party, she had been drunk, talkative, a toucher, fawning on people, seemingly quite happy in the way that drunks were until they weren't. Tobias and Amy had operated apart from each other that night, but Digger decided that parties were like that: one spouse clung to one group of friends and family, one to the other. The Manns had been like strangers that night, almost seemed to stay apart on purpose—from what Digger could remember (he had been drinking, too, of course)—but didn't they have words? Digger half remembered an incident, a word or two raised in anger, Amy's words. Could Tobias' wife be an alcoholic, alone at home all day, some nights, her disappointment in life and in herself leading to a violent, symbolic act? Following Tobias to the school, sneaking up on him in the office (he must have been doing papers or maybe scheduling), Amy Mann then shot her husband, emptied the gun on him, or maybe just stabbed him in the back with his own carving knife. That was what Anna did, wasn't it, one knife thrust straight to the heart? And Amy had had many more years with Tobias for resentments to fester, dreams deferred! Rotting, ripening into a plan. Digger added these sweet thoughts in lines from Amy's name, filling in one quarter of the page, and then he stopped: Amy didn't kill Tobias. He was blaming her because Anna chose another man and another life and stabbed him, Digger, killing him, Digger, leaving him in this half-life of waiting and hating. No wonder Detective Doyle seemed to consider Digger a suspect. From the little detective's angle, Digger's name would have been connected to the sad word "Despair."

But Digger knew that he didn't shoot or stick a knife into Tobias Mann, wondering at that moment how Mann was killed. Could he have been strangled? Was he bashed over the head? Shot seemed the most obvious. Or did the killer have Anna's aim and need just one mighty thrust? Or did rage take over and lead to multiple slashes? On TV, the victim was always shot or struck multiple times so that a cop would say knowingly, "This was personal," and the other cops would nod, one of them adding "The vic knew her killer" (or sometimes, but far less often, "his" killer). What did Doyle say? *Diagnosis pending.* If Tobias had been shot, stabbed, choked, bludgeoned, why would a diagnosis be "pending"? Maybe he was poisoned, and for a moment Digger imagined his old colleague's face purpled, a blue tongue protruding. Digger used coffee and sipped away that image. Of course, the cops would give away nothing that wasn't already destined for the papers. They wouldn't want suspects to have excuses for knowing specifics. Turning the page in his notebook, Digger made a bullet and then a question: How was Tobias killed? Digger decided to list any questions that arose and perhaps to speak to the little detective again.

Flipping the page back, Digger connected a line from Tobias to "Money," for that motive must always be considered with humans. From Money, he led to the word "Debt," and from there, he jotted "gambling?" What else could Tobias be into? Don't arrogant educators have hobbies like gambling on horses, a passion for the ponies? That thought led to mint juleps. But none of those images seemed right. Tobias never mentioned horses, or casinos, or sex parties, or mint juleps, but would he have done so? After over a decade knowing a man, Digger realized sadly that he never *knew* Tobias, that he never took the time to know him. Guilt bubbled up, formed a little pool, black.

Digger no longer drowned in those pools, not much, so he shifted his thoughts to students, to whether one of Tobias' students could have hated him enough to kill. *Students?* Although Digger got along well with his classes, he didn't keep in touch with any former pupils. Certainly, he would say hello to past students as he passed them on campus, and most of them would smile and greet him (some keeping their eyes averted). Did those averters hate Digger, want him dead? And Tobias was a harsher grader than he. Tobias Mann didn't even seem to like students. Could Tobias have destroyed an eighteen-year-old's dream, perhaps of becoming a writer? Wasn't there some student with a strange name—*North?* Jess, the secretary, told him that—a little office gossip, but what was it about? A grade probably, maybe a comment in class, but most likely a grade. Yes, North, and it was a grade, a simple "C," that set North off, the same North currently in Digger's 102 class: *George North?* How many Norths could there be? Digger had forgotten him because George just blended into the classroom's back wall and participated as little as possible, despite Digger's efforts. Could that same apathetic George North sneak into the Faculty Offices Building and shoot, choke, beat, or plunge a knife into a person over an average grade from last spring? *Only if he were crazy.*

Digger added these thoughts to his page, which had little room now, but he penned one more line from the center— administrators? Tobias had hated the administration, despised going to meetings, and complained about the school's reluctance to hire more full-time faculty, about the interference of *pencil-pushers* who never stood before a classroom, who had no idea what a teacher experienced or needed in way of support. Digger had no problems with any administrators, always finding them open to making room changes (at Digger's request) and even to adding a whiteboard to one room where Digger commonly taught. Of course, too, they would try to save money for the school. One of those men (they always seemed to be men) stood out in Digger's mind. From "administrators," Digger wrote "Omar Johns" because he remembered seeing Tobias and Johns having an unhappy-looking conversation some time ago, after a long meeting.

Maybe the butler did it, Digger smirked, realizing a sense of tiredness, contemplating a refill on his tepid coffee. Instead, to the "Tobias" center, he linked Dan Pinsky on the page although he added no corresponding link to any motive idea. Pinsky was the janitor, and Digger had always tried to avoid him and his endless comments and questions. Then he wrote "friendly with Tobias," "very religious," and "had opportunity," but that was as far as he got with any Pinsky motives. What other names would Detective Doyle add? He would look for a will, no doubt. Amy would supply that, so Digger flipped over the page and bulleted in another question: Who benefitted from the will? Could be as simple as that—the oldest motive in the world, money (or was that revenge?).

Digger gulped the last of the coffee (the donut was long gone), grimaced at its cold bitterness, and then added one more name directly from Tobias'—Paul Smith. Tobias had had to reprimand Paul for treating a student badly—was it for *striking* a student? That could not be it, or Smith would have been let go, but it was something dicey to do with Paul. Digger flipped the page and bulleted in "What did Paul do to the student?" Then he put a star next to that item because he would not ask the little detective about it. He would have to discover that answer himself.

Looking up from his notes, Digger noticed a police car out in the front parking lot. Smudged by the sun's glare, two faceless people appeared to be in the front seat, one head higher than the other, and suddenly Digger knew for certain that Detective Doyle had followed him, was watching him. Then Digger exhaled the paranoia and realized where he was: a donut shop. *Cops and donuts.* What could be more natural? Still, he no longer felt like sitting in the back booth anymore.

Digger thought of Simba at home, alone, her head no doubt resting on her short front paws, waiting for him. For that dog, Digger experienced a depth that echoed both love and loss. Five years back, Simba had started Digger's heart again, Simba and maybe the birds in his backyard, the breezes making silent melodies with the sea grass and with the stiffer limbs of his blue spruce, the gulls careening into soft sea landings, the pull of life, the earth's turning, but mostly Simba with her attentive eyes, soft woofs of agreement, gentle tail wagging, and need for Digger's presence. If Digger believed in anything, it was the life force labeled nature, all the non-human creatures, like Simba.

When Digger glanced up again, the cop car had disappeared. He looked down at the page. He had a small triangle of space left to the right of the central "Tobias," and Digger made a line to "Crime of Passion" because wasn't that common? Who would love Tobias so much that if they couldn't have him, then nobody could? No names came to mind. Before closing the notebook and getting up to leave, Digger stared at his main page, at the little connecting lines and the words—names and emotions—and wondered if his web had caught the killer. In the right corner of the page, unattached to his mapping, he had written one more word, "Anna." Why must those four letters still be inscribed on every page of Digger's life?

Chapter Five: Focus

> *Understand the three levels of focus because those ideas display your essay's or report's argument. The overall main one, your thesis, controls the entire paper's content; it represents your reason for writing. The next two levels apply to the composition's body paragraphs, the first being the topic sentence, the statement that focuses a paragraph's content and that directly points to and supports the thesis. One step lower, the third and final focusing step involves the supporting paragraph's structural points, which break the topic sentence down into specific manageable topics. In short, focus clearly.*

On the cancelled class day (both Monday and Tuesday were cancelled, just as the little detective had predicted, making for an extra-long Thanksgiving holiday), Digger had planned to work on focusing for the final project, and he decided to keep that plan on Wednesday for his eleven and noon Writing 101 classes and the later 102's. He hesitated, though, because this plan showcased a colorful roulette wheel he called Spin the Wheel of Organizational Choices. About the size of a large pizza, this wheel—perpendicular to the ground, held up by a wooden frame—revealed colorful pie sections, ten in all, which could be written on. Digger had found the wheel at a yard sale and immediately knew what he would do with it since he used to roll dice in class to determine organizational strategies for practice topic sentences. Now, if the wheel landed on yellow, then students would have to use *Illustration* as a strategy and create a topic sentence for a potential body paragraph; if it stopped on orange, then *Classification* would be the model topic sentences—on red, *Compare-Contrast*; on green, *Cause-Effect*; on purple, *Process*. He had these structural tactics written on the colored pie-shapes—each name/color twice. The wheel clicked as it spun. It was fun. And of course, that was the problem: the lesson seemed too enjoyable after Tobias' murder—too colorful and happy. However, Digger decided that OVC could use some color, especially since the faculty were all dressed up in dark clothes, mourning attire. The students, as usual, dressed as though August breezes played about the campus. In his first two Writing 101 classes, Digger's focusing lesson worked as expected.

In his first afternoon 102 class, Digger set the wheel down, and most of the students smiled because they had spun the wheel once before, earlier in the semester. Digger wanted to say something about Tobias and about the murder in general, but he had no text planned. Twice already he'd given off-the-cuff speeches, both different, both satisfying. He looked directly into the eyes of the 102 students, scanning faces. In the back row, George North's eyes stared back from an impassive façade. Digger felt jolted, then recovered.

"You all know what happened Sunday night," he began, and then he wondered why Amy Mann never contacted the police that night or the next day, a sudden thought that he wanted to add to his bulleted list of questions. All the students stared at him. Nobody was texting or checking their cell phones—not yet, anyway. "Some of you probably had Professor Mann," Digger continued, glancing to the back left to see George North's reaction, but Mann's former 101 student just continued to look back at him, expressionless. "And even if you did not, we should all take a moment to honor his life. A moment of silence."

Digger bowed his head immediately and hoped that students would do the same, that they would keep quiet and that no cell phone would chirp or buzz. Digger used to think that all students were the same, each generation, all mostly good with some bad habits, but he was no longer sure with the current generation, obsessed with cell phones, reluctant to talk in class, used to reading text messages and fragments, not longer, sculpted pieces of writing, accustomed to immediate information, to events covered in slang and superficiality, to news buzzed right into their pockets. He suddenly remembered a conversation with Tobias on this very subject, on Digger's summation of students. Tobias had declared that each new generation of student was definitely different: "worse and getting worser!" This memory evoked a trickle of guilt because Digger remembered thinking that Tobias was an ass at times.

Hearing a soft scuffle, Digger looked up at the back row, at George North, back-of-the-room George, who contributed nothing but mild distractions. Luckily, Digger had thought up to this point, George had not reproduced yet, although the two other guys in his row tended not to do much either. Short-haired (brown, manicured) with long bangs, white, smiles coming easily to their faces, George and his row looked like a pop band, and Digger could picture them swaying and swooning, delivering some awful melody in high voices. *George and the Hyenas, now playing.* At present, heads bowed, the class was still quiet, *thank God*, so Digger released them before they did it themselves. "Thank you," he said, adding "Professor Mann will be missed." Then he added, "Especially by me because somebody's going to have to take over as Chairperson and I don't want it to be me." Digger hadn't planned that; it just popped out. The students laughed and kept smiling, though, no doubt less at Digger's little joke and more at the chance to leave class early.

"By the way," continued Digger, "I hope that you all feel safe," and at that moment a gull swooped to the rooftop and screamed the typical three-note blast of a seagull, a blaring but attenuating honk. Everyone laughed at the juxtaposition of the word "safe" and the terrible sound, the screech and gurgle, including Digger. "The murder was a random act," he stated. "I have had a long talk with the lead investigator, and he says that the person is long gone, never to return (This was a direct lie since the little detective had told Digger no such thing, but

Digger imagined that the "fact" would help his students). Your dorms are all locked. You all have key cards, so nobody can get into your dorms. I would suggest, though, that nobody props open an outside door, just in case." The students all laughed again. *Probably nervous energy*, Digger decided.

Then he transitioned into the focusing exercise: "Okay, before the break, we started our last paper, a self-reflection of your skills, your improvements. We generated ideas using a table, so now we're going to practice focusing those ideas, creating clear, specific topic sentences. You know how this wheel works since we used it for Project Two. I'll spin first and then groups of three or four (we'll work in the current rows) will write a topic sentence that fits whatever organizational plan the wheel lands on. The best topic sentence earns the group three free minutes. Remember that I define 'best' the same way every time: clear and specific. And your TS needs to fit the plan from the wheel. It also needs to point clearly to your thesis, so I'll add a practice Project Four one on the board."

Digger turned to the white board, put "Practice Thesis" up near the top in green ink, noting that the green pens seemed to run out sooner than the blue or black or red ones, and began to write a thesis for the last paper: *I have improved...* Before he could finish the main point, he heard a loud male voice: "Let's practice with Professor Mann." *What?* he thought. "What?" Digger said.

He turned and faced the students, one of whom was standing and repeating his suggestion: "Let's practice with Professor Mann."

Digger had recognized George North's voice right away, even though he'd heard it so rarely, and he had asked the question "What?" just to buy himself some thinking time. Now, looking at the young man who could very well have killed his chairperson (*Shot him? Stabbed him? Poisoned?*), Digger did not care for the little smile on North's face. "What do you mean, George?"

"Let's write topic sentences about Professor Mann, about his killer. We can try to figure out who murdered him."

Digger immediately distrusted this idea, didn't want Tobias' death to seem like entertainment. He told the silent, attentive students some of this, the latter thought, looking at George and adding that thinking of Professor Mann was "thoughtful, though." Digger did not think that thoughtfulness had originated the idea.

Back-row-George, full of thoughts now, did not give up: "You could see the murder through a student's view. You could get some insight and tell your cop friend, the one who thinks the killer's long gone. We could help. Don't you want our help?"

Digger recognized manipulation when he read or heard it, but George was showing enthusiasm for the first time all semester—*and at least I've taught him how to use pathos*, Digger realized. Almost against his will, against his better judgment, in a short, clipped question, Digger asked the class, "What thesis would we use?"

A girl in the front row, Kristen—all the girls were named Kristen or Kirsten or Caitlyn, thought Digger irrationally— offered this: "How about 'Who killed Professor Mann?'" *That's not exactly a thesis*, Digger thought, looking about, seeing George's widening smile, the other students' nodding heads. "Yes," he heard one say, then "Let's do it!" from another. *A macabre crew.* Digger felt guilt climbing up his spine into his head, red guilt and fear. Yet the students' idea attracted him, too. Since Monday's brainstorming in the coffee shop, he had added lines, motives, and names to his notebook, especially more concerns involving Amy Mann. Seeing him hesitate, obviously pondering the topic switch, his students looked hopeful. But could this lesson twist open Digger to trouble?

"We would have to be respectful," Digger admonished, and the students all applauded. Then Digger gave a validation to the exercise, mainly to convince himself. "I must admit that I like looking at my friend's death from a student viewpoint. Maybe you people could help, could provide a different angle." In his mind Digger thought that his class would still be practicing focusing and planning, that to focus on Tobias would be a form of respect. He tried to sell himself the idea and half succeeded. Half was enough. As usual, when unsure, when brushed by embarrassment, Digger prattled on: "Remember that writers are objective. I've told you that all semester. Look at your topic from all angles, so I suppose that we should do this. Of course, 'Who killed Professor Mann?' is not a thesis, but that idea could work. It's an implied thesis, and the essay itself would lead to the answer. You might get some assignments like that. Okay."

Digger erased the "I have improved" thesis beginning and replaced it with "Who killed Professor Mann?" Then, before he could change his mind, he spun the wheel, which clicked and clicked in a nice solid way, slowed down, and finally stopped on a green pie: Cause-Effect.

"The perfect structure to help support our implied thesis," said Digger. "That means your TS needs to focus on reasons or consequences, not on both. That would be too much info for one body paragraph. Okay, let's go. A cause-effect body paragraph, so what would the topic sentence be? Work in your groups; teach each other. The best TS gets your group out three minutes early."

Digger shut up, reluctantly, and let the students work. He wanted to keep talking, maybe to justify what they were doing. He didn't want another teacher to walk in and see Tobias' name on the board or to hear them working on Mann's killer. Still, he did want to see what the students came up with. Would they focus on the wife? The groups all seemed to be conversing well, too—focused, huddled together, nobody on a cell phone. Digger felt uneasy but encouraged.

"Two minutes," announced Digger. "Get your TS on the board in two minutes for a chance to earn three free minutes," and this declaration got the class moving. One by one, a student emerged from each row (two rows on the right, three more on the left, with an aisle down the middle) and approached the board. Digger feared to look. Some students were writing too many words for the topic sentence to be effective, but that offered a learning lesson, he thought. "Every TS will help us, whether good or bad," he said as the students continued to squeak words onto the white board. "Every example helps us all." He didn't read the topic sentences yet; he was still a little bit afraid, apprehensive. As the young people wrote their groups' main focuses, Digger put the students' names on top of their creations, angling around the remaining writers, so that he knew who earned what. Finally, all the groups had added a topic sentence, hopefully for a cause-effect body paragraph, so Digger turned and one by one reviewed their efforts:

1. Professor Mann was a good teacher who didn't deserve to be killed.

2. A stranger killed Professor Mann for various reasons.

3. Since OVC lacks security resources, Professor Man was murdered.

4. Professor Mann was killed because he was in the wrong place at the wrong time.

5. The janitor did it.

Although Digger was annoyed by the last response, he then remembered that he had had the very same idea in the coffee shop, and the others offered some nice examples, two showing common problems involving the use of cause-effect.

He read all five topic sentences aloud, frowning when announcing the fifth one, which made the students laugh, then saying "Remember my warning about respect," which made the students go quiet. George North looked proud of himself, though, and Digger thought, *Damn it!* because 'The janitor did it' could fit cause-effect, but it mocked Tobias, mocked him. "For a cause-effect plan," Digger lectured, "the paragraph must be built around reasons or effects—plural—and although every topic sentence will have a cause-effect relationship with its thesis, not all of *these* TS's would lead to a cause-effect paragraph. For cause-effect, you need multiple reasons, and two of these TS's focus on just one reason apiece—which two?"

The students studied the board, and Digger enjoyed the way this active exercise led them to generate and compare examples, analyzing them, finding the problems. For that reason, he loved this spin-the-wheel lesson: it made his students work, but they had fun doing it. For a moment, Digger forgot his unease about using Tobias' murder as a teaching tactic. Gradually, a couple students pointed, and then one said "Three and four," and then others nodded in agreement. Digger had seen great analyses like this before, so again he pushed Tobias and guilt and fear away and just taught. "Exactly," he said. "The 'security' and 'wrong place' ideas are single reasons, and although every topic sentence will have a cause-effect relationship with its thesis, for a cause-effect body paragraph, you need multiple reasons that build the paragraph itself, and only one of these TS examples clearly could be broken into multiple causes—which one?"

George North said "Ours," and Digger automatically responded "Not yours." Two groups knew that they were out of the three-minute running, and one realized that their "good teacher" statement wasn't good as a topic sentence. Thus, when Digger eliminated the "janitor" idea, everyone knew the best TS was—the "stranger" one.

"Look," stated Digger, "this 'stranger' one announces its plan with the prep phrase 'for various reasons,' which tells the reader that he or she will see more than one reason why a 'stranger' killed Tobias—Professor Mann."

"Ours works, too," repeated George, undeterred, "because the janitor could have done it for various reasons. Just like the stranger."

"That's a good argument," admitted Digger, "so I'm giving your group one and one-half minutes because it could work. Your TS could lead to a cause-effect paragraph, but it could also lead to a Process body paragraph, a Process plan showing ways that the janitor did it."

"Like what?" asked George. "Like knifed?"

Like what? Digger again felt the prickle of irresponsibility, saw the image of a knife flashing by, and sensed the burning ember of anger growing. He knew that if he got mad at George North, then he would lose him for the rest of the semester, probably his cronies, too—the entire row. But the semester was almost over, and the anger was coming wrapped in righteousness, sweet and focused, the hardest kind to control. Digger tried, though, using a question.

"Why do you say a knife?"

"That's how he was killed," stated George North matter-of-factly. "With a knife. Somebody stabbed Professor Mann."

Digger felt stabbed, too. Was it true? How did George know? He sounded like he did know, but how? As if to answer him, George waved his cell phone: "It's in the news." Other students nodded their heads, making Digger think of bobble-heads. But maybe he was the bobble-head, for the students all seemed to know this new murder fact.

"Maybe I *should* get a cell phone," said Digger, and the students laughed because he had ranted against the phones periodically throughout the semester. The students' laugher calmed Digger down, turning the knife information from pathos (an emotional shock) to logos (a logical piece of evidence). "Okay," he continued. "The media has reported on this, but I don't want us to talk about it. We don't need to in terms of this focusing exercise, okay? In terms of your TS and a Process plan, the structural points would be ways, such as possible weapons, I suppose. If the TS's structural points were reasons, then those ideas would be completely different, such as 'envy' perhaps or 'revenge' for something."

"Why would a person knife another person?" George North had spoken and veered into the land of abstraction, a place Digger did not want to visit during this concrete lesson, especially since the little son of a bitch had mentioned the knife again. North had never participated in class like this, never been the star, yet he looked to Digger to be shining now. Digger thought of drugs. Then he imagined alcohol, a cold beer, the frost and foam, the golden peace.

"Money," he said. "Usually money, right? But we teachers don't make enough money for that to have been the motive."

Using the students' quick laughter and smiles, Digger transitioned to another spin of the wheel. "Okay, let's go again. I must say that I'm still not comfortable with our practice thesis, but I also never considered a stranger. I'm going to think about that."

"Maybe we could do our last paper on this topic." George North again.

"No, George," Digger laughed, not actually amused. "We will leave that topic to the cops. Okay, who wants to spin? Glenn, your group won three minutes last time, have a go."

Glenn, a short white boy who looked like a wrestler, had a go with the wheel, a solid spin that clicked madly and then continually and then methodically and then slowly to a stop: on yellow—Illustration. A paragraph built on examples. Digger felt a prickle of apprehension because this structural plan required specific ideas.

"Illustration," he announced, "so this paragraph will be built around examples of one narrowed topic. If the topic is too broad, then the examples will be too broad. The ideas will probably fit Classification, not Illustration, which requires direct evidence as its plan. Remember your purpose, our practice thesis. Narrow your topic." Then Digger added, "But be respectful with this topic. No sarcasm." Then he realized that in the past twenty minutes or so, he had not had to ask one student to put away his or her cell phone, that all those maddening instruments seemed to be off, forgotten. If this lesson ended up biting him, he could tell the disciplinary board about the absence of cell phones. Then Digger realized that administrators would not understand that distraction problem. Two minutes passed by in whisper-riddled silence.

"Two minutes," Digger announced. "Time's passing, so for a chance at three free minutes, get your Illustration TS on the board. Two minutes."

One person from the front right-hand row got up, Glenn again, and started writing, the words emerging into a statement: "Professor Mann was killed by one of his colleages." Digger noted the misspelling and whispered to Glenn in passing, "One of your words is hard to spell; there's a 'u' in it." Glenn went back to the board, and his group members said "colleagues." Glenn put the "u" in the wrong place, after the "a," so the two others laughed and corrected him until the sentence was all set. Glenn looked a little sheepish. Digger nodded at the finished group. *Maybe*, he thought of their topic sentence, *but that's a Classification TS*, a paragraph built around three or four people, multiple colleagues. *Not a bad try, though*, Digger decided, wondering why students always seemed to confuse Illustration and Classification.

As he was contemplating this, Kylie, a tall, pretty girl who looked like a volleyball player, approached the board (from the first-row group on the left), and her group's topic sentence appeared word by word: "Professor Man did not deserve to die." As she sat, looking pleased with the sentence, Digger thought, does anyone? Or does anyone deserve life? *Big questions.* Shifting his mind back to the tall girl's example, Digger realized that the TS didn't fit an Illustration pattern, that Kylie should have put that TS up last time because that's a Cause-Effect paragraph, the reasons why Tobias "didn't deserve to die." Maybe that TS could focus the final body paragraph in the essay, but then Digger remembered that his students would not be writing that essay.

Two more groups acted, sending their envoys, so that only George's group remained stationary. "C'mon George, Mike, Derrick. Time's almost up. Illustration's what you're after, a narrowed topic."

Two more topic sentences, hopefully good ones, began to appear before George moved. Apparently, he was his group's spokesperson and leader although North had never shown those qualities before, not even in small groups. Digger wondered how George had acted in Tobias' 101 class. He probably never said anything, especially since Tobias was more of a lecture and class discussion teacher. Digger had come to that conclusion from conversations with Mann throughout the years. Early in his teaching career, Digger had argued with peers about the need for more group work in class, for collaboration, but he no longer did so. Let teachers do what they want: that was his current motto. Digger no longer cared, not after Anna left him.

As George began to write a blue topic sentence, Digger read the third (a green one) and fourth (black) entries from the middle rows on both sides: "Professor Man was killed because he assigned too much homework" and "The janitor did it with a knife." Both attempts made Digger frown, especially the "janitor" extension idea, but he shook away the annoyance in order to look at the TS's objectively: The "knife" one was too narrow, although he supposed that the number of slashes could be evidence, but that was stretching it, and Digger decided that he would not mention that idea. The other one, though—too much homework? Evidence of that homework, specific assignments—that could work, and Digger was glad to see one winning TS on the board. Of course, that idea would mean that the killer was a student.

George passed him, saying "Another winner" to Digger, who looked up at the board at the fifth entry: "Professor Mann was killed because he was mean to students." Digger read the sentence in his head twice, concluding after the second time that this TS was in fact "another winner" and that this Tobias Mann work topic needed to stop. How could he explain the activity to administrators? Picturing his students brandishing carving knives and leering smiles, Digger realized that he needed to deal with these last examples and then end this murderous topic.

"Professor Mann was killed because he was mean to students," Digger read aloud. He didn't quite know what to say, evidence beginning to spin through his head. Tobias was definitely "mean" to students, as Digger himself had witnessed examples while in the Faculty Offices Building. Turning to his class, the teacher acknowledged that two groups would win round two, but that for the rest of the class they would all be switching to the last paper's topic, to *improvements* in their writing skills. Amidst the sounds of sadness and disapproval, of one trickle of laughter, Digger turned to the board and planned his questions for these five sentences. One was too specific, and two didn't fit the plan. Two could work, but both pointed to students—too much homework, too mean. Digger looked at the attentive faces and began to feel embarrassed. *Students and knives!* Digger wanted to erase the five sentences, especially the "mean" one, but he knew that he must soldier on. He must teach. Tonight, he would study his notes and relax with a beer or two, but for now he must teach.

"Okay, let's figure out who earns what."

Chapter Six: Free-Writing

When you're stuck, blocked, can't find a word to say or any pathway to a coherent topic, try what some call "hot penning," just letting the words roll across the page until the scratching turns into a workable thought, a plan, letting go of logic and searching for the unseen, for inspiration hidden beneath the tumult of a rational, conscious mind.

That night, light snow fell lazily on Ocean View, each flake taking its time and separate winding path to a sudden end on the grounds of the late Tobias Mann's estate. The hooded intruder sniffed the cool late-November air and liked the lack of scent, a promising blank canvas. The big tasteful house— white clapboard, of course—was lit on both levels, shining through the night like a cruise ship, but the stalking figure knew that she was alone inside—*the wife!* The Fox had been watching. Stealthy, wise, unseen, too quick for mortals, the Fox knew that light would not keep the wild at bay. Light always offered darkness a crack, an opening. The key was to nose persistently and relentlessly through the dark.

The crouching figure crabbed from tree to tree, shadow to shadow, and slipped behind an overgrown rhododendron bush that obscured one front window. *Not so tidy landscaping, Tobias. Very sloppy. You should have shaped up these shrubs!* The figure rose into a vertical line and stared into a comfortable, well-tended living room, for a moment seeing the glint of its own eyes, its own burning life force, twin flashes in the darkness, until its exhalations fogged the glass. If at that moment Amy Mann had looked out the bottom corner of that window, she would have seen a hooded head with no face, and the recent widow would have screamed.

Rich women all screamed. They screamed at a passing bee, at television violence, and even once the first victim, the great Mann, had told a story that his own wife had screamed at the milkman, who had just reached the side door when the paragon of domesticity had opened it to take out a small bag of trash. The scream had caused both humans to drop their burdens, a little parcel of coffee grinds and orange peels that stayed obediently intact and a quart bottle of milk that did not. Mrs. Mann had lambasted the humbled milkman—rightly so, the educator had informed his audience—and the rattled fellow had hurried to his van and returned with a complimentary quart "for your trouble." Professor Tobias Mann had laughed and laughed at that last line—*for your trouble*. He had repeated the sad salutation, his eyes gleaming. The other had not smiled, empathizing with the lowly milkman, but in those dual little shining eye lights he had seen the wild in the civilized man.

However, on this wintery night, Amy Mann did not scream, because she no doubt felt safe in the glowing house, her mind occupied by those difficult questions from Alex Trebek on Jeopardy. "Who is Gandhi?" she yelled at the television, but the hidden man heard Alex offer another Indian name instead. "Who?" said Amy to the lighted room and to herself, and the Fox heard her words as though they came from a different room, not from civilization into the night. *You need more insulation, Tobias.* Then the peeping Tom saw the wife take a long bracing sip—a gulp, really—from a heavy-looking glass full of amber liquid. *You should have put more money into these windows, Tobias. Perhaps some double-paned glass for your mansion. I can hear your wife fart out here, you know. The drunk woman who has forgotten you!*

Reaching up to push the window frame, to jimmy at the wood, the Fox imagined that the crystal glass would put a nice dent into the *mourning* woman's forehead. The creeper imagined yelling "Who is Gandhi?" as the heavy glass rose and fell. Thinking again that civilization always offered a crack, an invitation for the wild, the figure shuffled to the right, deeper into the shadows, turned the corner and ducked beneath the living room's side window, hearing the game show's signature tune: La la la la, la la la. ... Mann's monolith of a brick fireplace rose firmly and coldly into the sky, the fire extinguished. Beyond the brick tower, the thin Fox rose up, too, and peered into another room, Tobias' den apparently—all mahogany and male-looking, racks of leather-bound books on gleaming shelves reaching up to the ceiling. The room empty yet still lit—to keep Tobias' ghost away! *There are no ghosts, Amy, only wolves and foxes, only sheep and feral cats.* The den's windows refused to budge, too, and the next set led to a white and glaring kitchen. *Somebody must have a cleaning lady, probably an illegal immigrant.* Again, the windows remained frozen. For an instant, the Fox's brain exploded in frustration, but then the hood lowered and rested against the cold glass, the chest rising and falling, rising and falling, and the eyes rose up to watch the heavens tumble and crumble through the smothered darkness. The sporadic snowflakes looked like ashes. *Heaven's burning.* Inhaling deeply, the Fox reminded itself that its wiles, its patience, its ability to stop time and wait, those were the weapons of power.

The hooded figure moved to the back of the garage, dark, windowless, but with a door—locked. Neither of the heavy doors would rise either, each creaking and groaning in protest, little big metal ripping sounds in this muffled night. The Fox scurried back to another rhododendron. The bush's thick green leaves seemed to defy the cold, and the hooded figure felt sheltered, safe and secure. One more window gleamed above—an empty dining room, a crystal chandelier and candlesticks, other silver things. The Fox thought of the wonderful silver knife and reached into the grey sweatshirt's front pocket. *Amy, I have something for you!* But this last window also would not open. The snookered widow who stunk at game shows was locked up tight! Of course, glass could always be shattered. If the widow were to follow her poor husband into that deep, dark night, then the cops would look past OVC and into the Mann's private life, probably into their financial history. With any luck, children would become suspects—how many kids did Tobias have? The Fox pictured little Manns, but no number would stay in place.

Breaking glass would make noise, and the Fox was deceptive, not afraid but wary, smart. Would she answer the door? Would that *stupid, useless hussy* recognize the face framed in the peephole? Of course, she would peep out. Who would be so impertinent as to bother the grieving widow during *Jeopardy!* Neighbors could look out windows, too—all those *busybodies*. And maybe the widow was not alone after all. Maybe a goldbricking son or daughter rested upstairs, up in those lights. The Fox heard television applause. The show was over. Unfortunately, the widow had won, for now.

In an ungainly trot, the hooded figure hunched down the driveway, shifting further into the darkness, the heavens continuing to fall, shedding either fire or ice. *What's the difference? Both would kill.*

Chapter Seven: The Passive Voice

Here's some good advice about the passive voice: forget about it! Don't use it! The passive voice just means that your sentences' subjects have no clear doers. No one or no thing does anything. Sentences like that usually create wordiness and lack clarity, so although textbooks provide multiple pages on the passive voice and English teachers lecture about its use (i.e., when you want the doer to remain hidden, such as in science reports), do not read or listen to them. The passive voice just muddles clear communication.

The Faculty Offices Building, third floor, seemed empty, with a silence that pulsed, echoed, or at least dripped, like a church without a congregation. When he arrived that Friday morning at 10:30, Digger saw that the crime-scene tape was still crisscrossed against Tobias' closed office door, just two doors down from his own office, which still exuded a threat, too, as though the evil that had visited Tobias' room had spread and hidden. That first Friday after the murder, Digger's head hurt a bit—small waves of pressure. He stood in the doorway, looked at his desk, jammed up against the window in the narrow office—more like a closet, Digger had thought more than once—and decided to rearrange the furniture. Two words continued to swoop into his thoughts: students and knives. He no longer wanted his back to the door, so he moved one little bookshelf behind the door, knocking half the novels and old textbooks out as he dragged the shelf over, and then yanked his desk out to face the now open wall space. He moved the swivel chair back to the desk and sat down. Now he could turn left and see out the window (cloudy today, but no more flurries expected), turn right and see out into the hallway. Satisfied, he cleaned up a bit—papers and books set to right—and listened for his peers. *Were they all rearranging, too?*

Then he went to the 101 classes, ate a bag lunch, and then taught the 102 classes, feeling apprehensive about seeing the first one. After he returned to his office for his 4:00 to 5:00 office hour, Digger did some more thinking about George North.

As he sat in the waning daylight facing the wall, a seagull on the building's roof loosed a single guttural scream, and as usual the sound made Digger jump, at least inside. Those birds squatted atop the FOB roof all day, yelling at other birds and at nothing, at clouds. Yet Digger liked the noisy gulls because they, unchanging, somehow tethered him to time. Their bodies reminded him of white dinosaurs, and their attenuated calls seemed to connect the sea with the land and even the sky. He imagined their arcing shapes swooping above his black river inside, the dark trail at the bottom of his consciousness. That was where he pushed the shadows, buried them, but they didn't stay dead. They moved. His black river, its coiling dark waters always sliding past, whispering to him about insecurities and regrets. The Anna River, Digger sometimes labeled it, but the dark stream pre-dated his one-time wife.

In the ensuing ring of near silence, Digger heard a scraping, a dragging. *River sounds? What the hell is that!* He went to his office doorway and listened, located the scuffling sound up the hall, and stopped in the adjunct faculty office doorway. Paul Smith was busy rearranging the double office just the way Digger had that late morning. "Nobody wants his or her back to the door, I would imagine," Smith said, looking over his shoulder at Digger, and the latter imagined a stretched-out Quasi Moto, for his colleague didn't look well. *Looked hollow.* Staring at Digger, the old man explained his actions: "I heard you doing the same thing earlier. I looked in and liked your idea, so now no strange killers can sneak up on us with their pointy sticks."

Digger hadn't heard Paul Smith standing in his doorway earlier, or peeking around it, more likely, sneaking around the hallway, and that thought did not appeal to Digger. Neither did the "pointy sticks" comment because everyone seemed to know about the knife but him. "I thought you taught just in the morning, Paul. Why here so late?"

"Cleaning stuff out," Digger's old colleague replied. "Years and years' worth of stuff. I'm finally taking some action."

Digger understood procrastination: "I have too many books," he said to Smith. "Too many old textbooks that I don't use or even want. I'm going to do some spring cleaning, too."

"Spring," scoffed Smith. "Look out the window. Winter's coming, cold and breezy, sleet and snow. More like a winter wash, Digger." Smith had a deflated sort of look on his face, and Digger wondered again if he were sick. *Maybe cancer?* He looked thin and scooped out, sort of, even skeletal. Digger could almost smell the man. *Can't dogs smell cancer?* As usual, digger pictured Simba, her soft eyes and fur.

"How are you doing?" asked Digger. "How's the semester going?"

"Going, going, gone," laughed Smith. "Just a couple weeks left, thanks to Tobias and the vacation he gave us."

Digger decided not to mirror his colleague's cavalier attitude—probably a shield against anxiety, anyway. Digger conjured up another question, of Paul's wife—*what's her name, Debbie, Deborah, Donna*—but he didn't unleash it. In the past, when Digger had mentioned Paul's wife, the latter would inquire about Anna, knowing (Digger always thought and remembered now, too) that Anna was gone, had left him, and that Paul Smith was just sticking Digger with a knife.

That thought startled Digger, too, and he gazed anew at Paul Smith: an OVC lifer, part-time for thirty years at least, old fashioned in his teaching, probably tired of it all, eyeing retirement. Digger realized that he didn't really know Paul

Smith, that he didn't really like him much, either, that if he didn't share a career with the man, he would probably never even talk to him.

"You have even more crap than I do," Digger declared, realizing that he chose the word "crap" to jab his peer. The sticking felt both good and bad.

A grin broke across Smith's narrow face, and then he responded, "Life often gives us what we don't need and takes what we do." The hollow man waited for no response (Digger had none, had to agree with the dour philosophy, even admired the way his colleague put it) and resumed his redecoration. He dragged a four-row bookshelf toward the office door, exactly as Digger had done, and then used his foot to swing the door closed, right in Digger's face. To avoid being smacked, Digger actually had to step back a pace, and he was left standing stupidly before the closed door, expecting what? It to open? Apologies, a laugh or two shared? When nothing happened except muffled shuffling behind the adjunct faculty door, Digger moved back down the hall, away from his office and its stifling silence. Silence could gather and form, wait behind doors, and Digger imagined that happening within each office passed. All the doors were closed, but were they all empty? Even Jessica Williams was gone, just an empty desk at the corridor's end. Even the History Department's corridor, opposite his Humanities' one, appeared deserted. Fear blossomed and made Digger's skin prickle. Digger suddenly felt hollowed out, too, empty, a little lost: a passive spirit, a non-entity. He decided to start bringing Simba to work on a regular basis. He had done so periodically in past semesters. Out on the campus, students loved to stop and pet Simba, teachers, too, and usually Digger left his pup in his office during class. The thought of Simba then buoyed him now.

However, when he glanced back toward his own office, down the somewhat narrow corridor, he thought, *I'm looking through the eyes of the killer.* The killer stood here, listened to this same silence, maybe even at this exact moment five days ago. Where did he come from? Why Tobias? Who would kill an English teacher? How many times was Tobias stabbed? Nobody seemed to know that answer, and Digger had bulleted the question into his notebook. Digger decided that Tobias must have been targeted because why else would a person even go to the Faculty Offices Building, especially on a holiday weekend? Because almost no one was on campus or at least around the office buildings—that answer seemed obvious to Digger now. But how did the killer know that Tobias had come to work in solitude? His wife would have known. Amy? *His wife did it*, Digger decided amidst an emotion containing some joy. *Just like mine*, and his lips actually curled downward as he slipped on the dark path's wet leaves and slid into the black river that ran just beneath his conscious thoughts. *The only difference is that Anna struck deeper, so deep that the weapon disappeared right into my back.* A crime without a clue, without a victim—or at least a dead body.

Dismissing this thought as melodramatic, Digger discovered that he was standing still, stiff and listening. *What did the killer hear?* Probably just a gull or two, soaring about and asserting their twilight opinions. *Did Tobias make noise?* His door would have been open; it always was, and light would have been shining out. It was dark, Digger realized suddenly, the murder happening after darkness fell on Sunday night, after 5 o'clock or so. The killer saw Tobias' light from outside. That was how he (or she, *Amy?*) knew. The killer simply followed the light. Tobias must have arrived while it was still daylight and so not switched on the hall lights. Then darkness came, but he had switched on his office light anyway, to dispel the shadows. Unless he were just grading papers, his computer would have been humming, his key strokes making muffled tapping, the beast approaching on softly padded feet. Digger pictured light shining out into a dark hallway.

He walked quietly down that hallway, passing the adjunct faculty door but hearing no noise, as though Paul Smith had left, yet the hollow man could not have passed Digger unseen. *What was he doing in there?* Digger wanted to knock, half raised his right arm, when from the other end of the hall, a voice beckoned, made Digger's muscles tighten and freeze. *The janitor did it*, thought Digger irrationally, for he knew Dan Pinsky's booming vocals, his inappropriate and forward statements.

"Hey, what are you doing in here?" Dan Pinsky had declared.

Fighting the urge to yell that he worked here and slip away, to slink into his office and close the door ("Have lots of work to do!"), Digger steeled himself against the advancing social storm.

Even without November's late-afternoon shadows, without a murder scene four doors down an empty hallway, Dan the Janitor always unnerved Digger, turned him into an object through sheer verbiage, rendered him a sounding board (*just like my mother*, thought Digger), a wilted plant, for Dan always sounded clear and sure and rooted to the earth so firmly—or to the sky, to Heaven. Around this uneducated maintenance man, the multi-graduated Digger mumbled his replies, his words sounding weak and ragged even to him. Dan often didn't seem to hear words.

"Did I scare you?" beamed the approaching man, and the smile on his round face suggested that he hoped so. Digger expected to hear that God was watching him, for Dan Pinsky often mentioned the Lord. A big man, standing over six feet, all of them fully fleshed, the janitor was not so much fat as slightly rounded but solid. He reminded Digger of a professional wrestler (the one destined for pinning), his mop a prop, but Dan pummeled his adversary only with verbiage: "You have office hours now? Where are all the students? They don't want extra help? They always wanted help from Professor Mann. He had a line out his door of students. He was always in demand. A God-fearing man. He who stabbed Professor Mann will find his judgment."

Digger wanted to argue, to say that God didn't do much to help the man, that he never saw a single student visiting Tobias, and that if a student did, it would have been to complain about a grade or about a confusing assignment. Digger wanted to argue that students never came to office hours anymore anyway because of email, that office hours were archaic, a waste of time, that this conversation was a waste of time, and good bye to you! But all he said was this: "I'm going to miss Tobias."

That realization surprised Digger, and Pinsky, too, seemingly, because the big man closed his mouth. He stared at Digger, his fingers tightening around the mop handle, and then looked toward Tobias' door, all wrapped up. Digger thought of all the empty rooms and wondered again if they were all actually empty. What was Paul Smith doing in there? He wanted Paul to come out and draw away the big janitor, but nothing happened. The silence ticked by, heartbeat after heartbeat.

Dan Pinsky, Dan the Man, of course—as people had yelled and laughed all his life, no doubt—started up again. "The cops have that room all closed up. They don't want me to clean in there. But I made a list of suspects. You were on it. I put all the professors in this hallway on the list, but I crossed most of them off. I crossed you off right away. You liked Professor Mann, you talked to him. He liked you, too, and he felt bad about your wife leaving you. He told me that. Professor Mann told me many things. He took the time to talk, every day. He said, 'Poor Digger,' more than once, too. And he told me that you would be a good chairperson, that you should take over for him. He didn't like the paperwork. He didn't like other professors complaining about things, like their schedules. He thought they should be more grateful, God willing, but that's not how people are. The Lord knows. I'll tell you one person he didn't like at all, that Professor Domberg. He called him an 'arrogant bastard'—can you believe that? He told me that and more. He thought that Domberg should 'keep his mouth shut.' That's what he told me—'arrogant bastard' and 'keep his mouth shut.' That's why Professor Domberg's still on my list, and so are two other teachers. That Smith guy, the old one, he's on there because he's a shifty devil. He never stops to talk. Professor Mann thought so, too. The Lord will judge, His will be done."

Upon hearing "that Smith guy," Digger wanted to reach out and shush Dan Pinsky, Dan the Man, because he knew that Paul could hear his booming words (people in passing airplanes probably could), but as usual the torrent of statements overwhelmed and crushed him, beat him down. If only Digger could sink down into the floor and reappear elsewhere, a different world, a Dan-the-Man-less place, and he thought again of his dog, wished that he had brought Simba to work today.

"I have seven people still on my list," Pinsky continued, "and one's the killer. Three teachers, one administrator, one student, and then just a stranger, a madman. That's who the police want us to think killed Professor Mann. That way they don't have to do any work. Professor Mann thought that some of the part-timers were like that." Pinsky leered to punctuate his point, making his fat face even uglier, thought Digger. Dan was clearly pleased with his analysis, and despite himself and his creeping desire to melt away from the present, Digger felt drawn into the janitor's list of seven: three professors— *obviously Don, Paul, and who else?*

"What other professor's on your list?" Digger asked, his voice clear now because he really wanted to know.

Dan the Man clearly liked questions. He sort of puffed up and very deliberately placed his mop against the wall as though to answer he would need both hands, that analysis so deep required wild gesticulations. Then, somewhat unclimactically yet chillingly, Dan the Janitor nodded his head to the right.

"That's the adjunct faculty office," said Digger. "A dozen different teachers use that room. Which one's on your list?"

Pinsky rarely had so captive an audience, so he didn't need to ensnare with words. He seemed to recognize the drama of silence. He leaned forward now, and Digger found himself actually holding his breath, so he breathed. "The Jezebel!" stated the big man suddenly, following quickly with "Bonner. She hated Professor Mann. I heard her complaining about him in there," and he pointed to the door, one arm extended accusingly like the Ghost of Christmas Yet to Come. In spite of this mad claim, Digger shivered. The maintenance man continued: "She was saying that Professor Mann didn't care about part-timers and he used them. He made them wait for their schedules and didn't respect them. He was old. He was a bad teacher." Pinsky had mimicked the last two statements, trying to sound like a complaining woman. Then the janitor scoffed loudly, and the sudden noise made Digger jump—but just inside. "That Jezebel said that she would leave the school if she could. She was mad, mad enough to kill, but she will have her reckoning. Thou shall not kill."

Digger wanted to stand up for Elena. He knew that she didn't kill Tobias (*right?*) and didn't like the word "Jezebel," didn't quite understand it. "Elena Bonner couldn't kill anyone," he told the big man, "especially with a knife. She works too hard, for one thing. She's got classes here and at the community college, where they load in the students." That thought got Digger thinking about Pinsky's list again. Since the big man failed to respond to his Bonner argument, Digger asked, "Which student?"

Dan was not done with the teachers, though, and Digger's point about Elena seemed to have missed the mark. Pointing to the door, Pinsky stated, "They all envied Professor Mann. He was at the top. People listened to him, respected him, wanted to be in his office. He was a real professor, not like some, not like that part-timer. And the students respected him. They would line up outside his door. None of the rest have students like that. They would line up outside his door, all the time."

This was old news to Digger, who had learned it five minutes earlier from Pinsky himself, but still jealousy ignited in his brain, just a little flame, a pilot light. He strongly desired to tell the big man that these endless students were complaining about Mann, not worshipping him, or that they were confused by Tobias' assignments, which were confusing, from what Digger remembered of them, not much. But Dan was off again, saying something about the "Head teacher. Anyone would kill to get what they want, right? Anyone."

"What could they get with Tobias out of the way?" Digger asked that question mainly to himself, but Pinsky grabbed it and off he went: "Respect. Prestige. The Head Man. The office! Professor Mann's office was twice as big as all these other closets. Especially the part-timers' office—look how they're all crammed in there! They make a mess. They all want full time, too, and now there's an opening. Who will be in Professor Mann's office next semester? That's what I want to know. God willing." Pinsky's summation ended with a smirking silence. Dan the Man created a large presence; his breathing sucked most of the oxygen from the air.

About the big office, Digger didn't know, had no idea. He found himself looking at the big man's big brown shoes, but not really seeing them. Tired, thirsty—*yes, thirsty*—Digger wanted again to be alone and thought with relief that it was Friday. He just had to get away from this current situation. Then he thought of weakness, of power, of Tobias' empty office. Digger had assumed that Don would be Acting Chair by next week, probably full chair over winter break. Don seemed like the logical choice: with his trimmed brown beard and take-charge manner. When the crime-scene tape was cleared away, Don would move in. But would a part-timer be raised to full-time status to fill the open slot? Would OVC go in-house or seek someone new—or fill the slot at all? Maybe the administrators would just save some money. The faculty union wouldn't like that. All the adjunct faculty had to be thinking of Mann's death as an opportunity—a disquieting thought. Digger had not felt the part-timers' angst in a decade, had somewhat forgotten the anxiety around scheduling time. Could such mental turbulence lead a man—or a woman—to kill?

Pinsky appeared to take Digger's non-answer as proof of his argument, which he continued again, repeating his question about Tobias' office, casting his accusations up and down the seemingly deserted corridors, down through Humanities and across into History, closed for the present. Suddenly, Digger realized that he and Dan were on a stage, beneath the lights, the unseen audience rapt yet hidden in shadow, and he wondered if Detective Doyle had interviewed the janitor. He pictured the little man and the big one together, almost chuckled at the juxtaposition. But now Pinsky's list of seven was probably in the little detective's computer: Don, Paul, Elena, the Stranger, and two other names—an administrator and a student, and who else? That was just six; Dan had mentioned seven suspects. He had miscounted, apparently, or maybe Digger was still listed.

Digger had thought of Bill Jacobs first, but he wasn't on Pinsky's list. That seemed strange. Bill must talk to Pinsky, must give him time. They were probably complaining buddies. Was Bill on Doyle's list? Bill Jacobs, obnoxious to everyone with his right-wing views, odd with those blazing eyes, and a rotten teacher, to boot. Yet still Bill could squeeze empathy from Digger's chest because the complaining man had no answers for his sorrows. When everyone else was to blame (students, peers, administrators, Democrats), then there was no hope of change. Bill could have reached a boiling point, saw his life played out, the end like the present, saw Tobias as an enemy, a co-conspirator in his life's misery. Digger clearly saw the motive and thought again about Doyle, about the added weight of police suspicion, too. And then he thought of George North. To mention him to the little detective would be ludicrous. How could Digger explain that suspicion? He pictured sitting in the detective's one office chair: "You see, George never participates in class, but he wanted to create topic sentences about Tobias, and he smirked a lot, too." Thinking of that class, Digger suddenly remembered another topic sentence: "The janitor did it."

Digger looked up at the big janitor and realized that the man had stopped talking. His mop held like an old musket, Pinsky was just staring at Digger as though expecting an answer, but Digger had not heard any recent question. *Dan's probably rethinking my innocence*, thought Digger. *He's going to go home and uncross my name.*

"It won't be me," said Digger, suddenly remembering the conversational thread, Tobias' office. Digger imagined his words sailing off down the hall, because they came out louder than he had anticipated. He pictured the words flapping against the closed doors, breaking apart, crumbling, words becoming November's dead brown leaves. The silence seemed louder now. "Dan," he argued, "nobody would kill Tobias Mann in order to become chairperson, that's an elected position. We all choose the chair. And who would kill out of envy?"

This question, a complete contradiction of the other's argument, apparently rendered Dan the Man mute, for his mouth stayed closed as his eyes shifted a bit, landed on his mop, and then the big man plucked it up and moved past Digger, mumbling one final statement: "The Lord's list is the one that matters. That list holds the right name and the judgment." Digger watched him stop before Tobias' door and stare at it. Then the janitor started to work, swishing the mop from one side of the hall to the other, big arcing waves, but he cast a look over his shoulder once, and then twice, to glance at Digger and to think in silence some more. The blessed silence offered an escape.

After Digger slipped into his own office and closed the door, he could still hear the mop, swoosh-swoosh, and imagined Dan Pinsky's efforts outside the dead man's door, rubbing away the sneaker prints of all those devoted students, polishing the entranceway to the shrine of one man, envied by all, who repeatedly took the time to communicate with a janitor who knew it all.

Chapter Eight: Rhetorical Questions

In an essay, if you ask a question, don't answer it. Don't say "Yes" or "No," because doing so will make your prose sound too informal (too conversational) and your thinking uncertain. A question should have a rhetorical purpose, the answer transmitted to the reader through the interrogative itself. In short, in an essay, a question should actually function like a strong statement.

After Monday's afternoon 102 classes, in one of which George North again participated well, not mentioning Tobias at all, but smiling oddly (at least to Digger's mind). Digger saw Bill Jacobs leaving the Faculty Offices Building, head bowed. He yelled to him, and Bill waited for Digger to reach him.

"I haven't seen you all semester, it feels like," said Digger. "How's it going?"

"I'm a morning man, and it's going, same as always," declared Bill Jacobs, another tall, slightly stooped fellow, like Paul Smith, but this one with a big brown beard and big blazing eyes, more energy. Digger had always thought that Bill looked like a preacher from some far-away land, maybe Montana. He seemed to burn inside. "Just trying to teach these little asses how to write a sentence," continued Bill, eyes wide and shining. Picturing little curls of grey smoke rising from his peer's ears, Digger remembered that he didn't really enjoy conversations with Bill Jacobs and that maybe this bearded son-of-a-bitch was a killer.

Already, Digger wanted to change the conversation, so he said what everyone had been saying: "What do you think about Tobias' death?"

Bill didn't hesitate or filter his responses: "He deserved it." The stooped man laughed once and stared at Digger as though willing him to say differently, then turned and, bowed slightly forward, as though pushing against a wind, ambled off. Watching his old peer's exit, Digger wondered why the morning duo of Bill and Paul were invading his late afternoons. He yelled "Don't we all?" to Bill Jacob's back, and then bid his old colleague adieu. *That guy's nuts*, Digger mused, climbing to the third floor, finding the secretary's desk vacant, and making his way down to his office, down the killer's row as he now thought of that journey.

His office seemed different somehow—cleaner? Maybe it was just the rearranged furniture, the discarded books. Maybe the cops had rifled through his work life, looking for (what?) the knife, a bloody towel, a signed confession. But maybe it was the little hole created by Tobias' passing, by the past's rear-ending of the present. *Death does that*, thought Digger: *keeps bumping its cold nose into you. Reminders that nothing's the same. Did we all deserve it, though?* Digger wondered if the police had searched everyone's office, or just his, of if he were just imagining their intrusion. He imagined the little detective nosing about, pulling out his files and drawers. Could the police do that? Digger didn't know, assumed that they could.

Seated at his fairly organized desk, some notes and papers scattered about, he again wished that he had brought Simba to school, vowed that he would from now on, and then he thought of Bill Jacobs and Detective Doyle again, of responsibility, of false accusations, of leaving this murder to experts and forgetting it, moving on. Why did he have so much trouble moving on? He thought of Anna, of the black river. Guilt was like blood: it moved slowly, dripped, nourished, and in death it turned black. A stain impossible to erase.

Impulsively, Digger checked the white section of the yellow pages (*who does that anymore!*), dialed *9* to reach an outside line, and then called the OVP, asking for Doyle, who with one quick click greeted him coldly (or just flatly), almost as though he'd expected the call, was waiting with his hand over the phone. However, the detective said that he would be "pleased" to see Professor Diggerson and that 5:00 today would be "acceptable." Digger wondered whether he was making a mistake.

After the short conversation, Digger swiveled in his chair for a bit, pondered Doyle's abrupt response (was it a trap?), considered the word "pleased" (the myriad reasons for pleasure), listened to the empty corridor (not even the adjunct faculty door had been open), glanced at Wednesday's lesson plans (no changes needed), and wondered why Don Domberg had not been announced as the Acting Chair yet (Did the administration suspect Don?). He looked at the darkened computer screen yet left the machine off. He brooded about being elected Acting Chair himself, about all the extra duties and meetings. Would he want the extra power, the responsibility? Another rung on a ladder that no longer interested Digger, who had reached his goal as a full-time tenured faculty member and who no longer had many other dreams. Halfway through his office hour, he gave up and exited the building, for who was there to reprimand him?

The late November air felt good—clear and crisp, quieting the gulls for a change. Fat white clouds sailed slowly far above, below the blue canopy, and Digger saw students on distant paths but passed nobody as he navigated between three-story brick buildings on the way to his truck. That solitude was not uncommon for a late afternoon. Even at a private school, where the students often hailed from distant states, the young jumped ship often, especially on the weekends, going who knows where? To Boston, New York, back home to Connecticut, maybe, if license plates offered any answers. A couple spaces from Digger's truck, a cop car had been parked, illegally. It was empty, and looking about,

Digger spied no policemen. He wondered if the car had followed him to school late this morning.

At the station, Officer Jowles had been replaced by a pretty female cop, Officer Tanner, who apparently had received training in dealing with the public (unlike Jowles), or who'd not worked long enough to be jaded. She actually escorted Digger down the hall, and Digger experienced the warmth of her close presence and then the cold when she deposited him at Doyle's closed door: that odd déjà-vu, that same feeling of being sent to the principal. He glanced back down the short hallway to see Tanner's face turned his way. "Just knock," she called, and Digger smiled. He had a sudden thought: *Don't the killers always try to get themselves involved in the investigation?* Won't Detective Doyle suspect Digger and his motives? *Too late now*, Digger realized, and he knocked twice on Doyle's door, picturing Officer Tanner's smile, too.

Hearing the accustomed "Yes," Digger felt tempted to wait, to knock again even, forcing the little detective to stand up and open the door, revealing his stature. Last time, when Doyle had risen to usher Digger away, the cop had only half stood, crouched, masking his height, it had seemed to Digger. Glancing back at Officer Tanner, Digger found her eyeing him. "Go in," she stated, and she smiled again. Feeling foolish, Digger obeyed, and there was Doyle, seated and comfortable, confident, with darkish eyes (maybe brown) that gave nothing away—a poker player's facade. Had they shaken hands last time? Digger could not remember, but this time the detective reached out and presented Digger with a single firm pump, like an old friend, and Digger remembered the fast, professional grip from last time. *He's trying to put me at ease but to still show his superiority*, decided Digger, who reached an unsettling conclusion: *I'm a suspect. I'm the enemy.*

Digger was not sure what to say, so he started by stammering a bit. "Thank you for seeing me again and on such short notice. I …" *I what? I suspect a friend and a student?*

"Take your time," countered the little detective, and the half-smile seemed honest. "You have something to tell me? You suspect a colleague, but you don't want to name him? You think we'll charge off and harass the man?" Doyle's voice rose just a bit near the end of each statement—on "tell," "name," "harass"—but Digger recognized that the short man was not asking him questions. He knew why Digger had come back. Who else had come back?

"I had a conversation with a staff member," replied Digger slowly, "and he had some suspects. I wonder if you've talked with our maintenance man, Daniel Pinsky. He actually knows quite a bit, talks to everyone, always has his eyes open. He has a list of six suspects."

The little detective smiled again on this day of miracles, said, "We have interviewed Mr. Pinsky. He seems to feel strongly about religion as the solution. On this earthly plain, he gave us many opinions and names, more than six. About the only name not on his suspect list was yours, Professor Diggerson. He said that you don't have it in you to kill someone."

That's nice, thought Digger, realizing that he'd been holding his breath. *Not a suspect*, and was Doyle actually joking with him? Did he say "earthly plain?" To be considered innocent made a real difference. To be a person with whom others joked. Digger smiled back at the policeman, but then paranoia crept in again. "I wasn't sure about contacting you," he continued. "I know from TV that murderers sometimes try to get involved in their own investigations. I didn't want you to think I was doing that."

The happy little fellow grinned again—at least two more smiles than Digger had received last time—but he didn't respond with more encouraging or humorous words.

"The thing is," Digger continued, feeling the silence, "Pinsky's list didn't contain a name that mine does. I also made a list of suspects. That's what I do to generate ideas, as a writing teacher, I mean, I make lists. Then I connect my ideas with lines, looking for relationships, usually in order to build body paragraphs, but this time to find a killer." The word sounded melodramatic to Digger.

Doyle just responded by saying that he'd like to see Digger's list, but now that the point had arrived, Digger felt a little protective of Bill Jacobs, his main reason for coming back to the station. "Innocent until proven guilty," announced Digger absurdly, reluctant to accuse a peer, a friend, sort of, the only kind of friend Digger had anymore (except for Simba). "You see, when I first heard—when you told me about—Tobias' death, a name flashed through my mind. I have absolutely no proof, and Dan Pinsky didn't suspect him, but one of my colleagues has some anger issues, and he's directed that anger at Tobias Mann on occasion, about scheduling and teaching tactics. And he has guns, I think, and probably army knives, because he's told me about the Gulf War, the first one, the more ethical one. Anyway, when you informed me of Tobias' murder, I thought of him. To me, he seems capable of violence, a sort of caged rage, and I don't think that way about any of my other peers."

"His name?" requested the little detective, and Digger noticed the command in the question, though Doyle's patience seemed intact, as though the detective always remained controlled and analytical. Digger liked to think of himself that way.

"No proof," he responded, "but I think you should investigate Professor Jacobs, Bill Jacobs. He's not a happy person, and he's impulsive, gets mad if you disagree with his views. He's a Republican, very much a Republican, as far right as you can go before meeting the Gestapo."

Digger didn't know how the other would respond, somewhat expected him to say that being a Republican was no crime (then the two could chuckle and say, "but it should be!"), but Doyle surprised him with his next question/statement: "Do you think this was a crime of impulse?" And Digger realized that he was being directed, taught, for of course it was not a crime of impulse. It was planned, calculated.

"No," admitted Digger. "Not an impulse. It was a calculated plan. And you would make a good teacher, Detective Doyle."

The little detective deflected the compliment: "Who else is on your list, Professor Diggerson? You did not come down here just to tell me about Jacobs. And we have interviewed him, by the way. That's no news. We have interviewed every faculty member from the Humanities Department. What I garnered is that teaching is more competitive than I realized. The adjunct faculty, part-timers, they are *part* time in name only. They teach more classes, albeit at different schools, some at three different colleges, than the full-timers like yourself. Among that group—the adjunct faculty—considerable negative feelings exist."

"Are any of the part-timers suspects?" asked Digger, but the detective only smiled, a thin, toothless grin. No names would pop out from between those lips.

"Who else is on your list, Professor Diggerson? I'm interested."

"Well," said Digger, thinking of the adjuncts but keeping the conversation going, "now that I'm here wasting your time, I might as well spill all of my suspicions—if you have time."

When Doyle nodded that he did, Digger continued: "I wonder about Tobias' wife, Amy. Tobias never talked about her, never said nice things or called her from the office (that I could tell). He once made a disparaging remark about marriage, in response to my own, to my past marriage. And they fought once at a faculty Christmas party, sort of a nasty confrontation, quick and harsh like a pair of cats." Digger paused, wondered if he should have made that comparison (but he liked comparisons), started in again. "What really makes me wonder about Amy is that she must not have reported Tobias as missing. You said that our secretary, Jessica, called you that Monday morning. Why didn't Amy

Mann call you the night before? Why didn't she report her husband as missing if he went out and never came home?"

Digger realized that his body had inched forward even further, that his face was now fairly close to the little man's, that now *he* was asking questions that were in fact statements, but Detective Doyle did not respond, just looked at Digger, waiting.

"Mrs. Mann is not a suspect at this time," he finally said into the wordless void. "This should remain between us, Professor Diggerson. We thought along your lines at first, but his wife has been cleared. Mrs. Mann had her reasons for not contacting us Sunday night, which I will not get into here. Those reasons support her innocence."

Digger understood, and he shook his head to show it—*no, no, of course*—but still he would have liked to know those reasons, locked away in the detective's head and computer. The little big man had confided in him, drawn him closer, and Digger felt a surge of warmth almost immediately doused by suspicion: *This cop's playing me. I'm just a mouse.* Digger wanted to roar, to ask for the reasons that supposedly supported the wife's innocence, any wife's, and that sweet suspicion made him remember Tobias's will, one of his bulleted questions from the coffee shop. He realized, though, that Detective Doyle would never answer his questions.

Thinking about an exit and then about George North, Digger leaned forward and started to grimace a bit, but then he stopped himself, shifted to his other topic. "I'm wasting our time, Detective Doyle, but I have one more name, a student, and my reason's sort of silly." Digger hesitated, received a nod, continued: "One of my students, George North, was in Tobias' Writing 101 class last semester, and George complained about Tobias' grading. That's not uncommon. All students complain about English teachers' grading. I heard this second hand, though, from our secretary, Jessica, and now George is in my 102 class, and normally he doesn't try very hard; you'd hardly notice him, but this past week he made comments about Professor Mann. He seemed interested in his murder, mentioned the knife. He seemed to want to get involved in figuring out who killed him."

"That sounds familiar," said Doyle, dead-pan, and when Digger caught on, he laughed, a little uneasily, though, just a pair of *ha*'s, because Doyle's half-smiling face remained more closed than open.

"I know, I know," said Digger, plowing onward, using words to cover his disquiet: "I just wondered if you'd checked out any students who had grievances with Tobias. Records might exist. If George had strong words with Tobias, it would probably still not be written up, but maybe. And maybe George North has a juvenile record."

"You think like a detective, Professor Diggerson. And now I need to get back to being one. Thank you for your thoughts and your information. You've given us some questions to answer. Feel free to contact me with any further suspicions. We take all tips seriously, especially when it comes to murder."

That sounded melodramatic to Digger, who recognized the professional dismissal. This time the little detective remained seated as Digger rose, thanked the other man, and departed, a little sheepishly. He had expected a parting handshake, but the other man's mind was already beyond Digger, or seemed to be. In the hallway, Digger stretched his arms and legs, which were all stiff. He noticed sweat trickling down his back, and he felt a sudden urge to hide. That urge was not uncommon for him. Then he took a step, and that got him going, both body and mind. Wondering about records and hidden motives, about George North's sudden leadership qualities and Detective Doyle's height, Digger remembered nonetheless to say goodbye to Officer Tanner.

Chapter Nine: Unity

Students have trouble understanding this term, which simply means oneness, a repetition of and reference to the focusing topic so that the content all points to that one idea. Without unity, your paragraph forces readers to stumble through your scattered thoughts no matter how strong and specific the content.

A dozen days after Tobias Mann's murder, random mainly murder-centered thoughts still abounded across Ocean View College's campus:

From Kate Timmons, one of Digger's students: "I heard the janitor did it!"

From George North: "Somebody stuck it to the Mann."

From Dan Pinsky: "Professor Mann was the smartest man I ever knew. He talked to me about everything. None of the others can take his place"

From Omar Johns, one of many administrators: "We have to replace him soon. Just a temporary replacement before a formal vote. Whom should we move up?"

From another administrator: "Should we be allowing that dog on campus, Diggerson's dog? What if it bites somebody?"

From a member of Campus Security: "Nobody who should not have been on campus Sunday night was on campus. Nobody got through us."

From Jesse Williams, secretary of the Humanities Department: "I will never walk down to that room again!"

From Don Domberg, Head of Tutorial Services: "Tobias was tough and stubborn. We didn't often see eye to eye, but I respected him. I did. OVC will never be the same. If called upon, I will try to make Tobias proud."

From Detective Doyle to a colleague (outside the Faculty Offices Building): "I get the feeling that nobody liked this guy."

From Doyle's colleague in response: "Except that whack-job janitor!"

From Digger to various teachers: "When's the funeral?"

Since his meeting with Detective Doyle, Digger had played the scene repeatedly in his mind, always leading to the fact that the policeman suspected him of the killings. It all traveled back to that accident, to that big mistake, one case of drunk driving, and Digger bitterly re-enacted that old crash, obsessed about its cause, the loss and emptiness and injustice that ended up with his nice old pickup wrapped around a pole.

Ironically, the alcohol he'd consumed had kept him safe that night, had limbered his body and prevented his bones from breaking, but since then he'd been tainted. Blame came more easily: blame for the DWI, for the loss of his wife (not often did he blame Anna—until around the fifth beer). Blame for anything could attach itself to Digger like a cancer, a black spot that darkened all issues and magnified his own culpability. Deep down, though, usually between the second and third beer (in whose foamy realm he could become the victim), Digger knew that he was not to blame for Anna's departure, that if anything they both were, or youth was, yet logic could not often hold against the poking taunts of emotions, not always, not usually. According to his mother, the world was getting younger, and if that were true, then more mistakes waited to be made. Was Anna getting younger without him? *Where did the line between old and young wait?*

he wondered, and he imagined himself to be on that threshold: the age of 41.

He still wished to blame the wife—in this case, Amy Mann. Repeatedly, he returned to Detective Doyle's assertion that she was innocent. How could the police have determined that? She could have hired a hit man, as unlikely as that seemed, but wasn't everything about Tobias' murder unlikely? Digger thought of all the murder victims in America and realized that most were either powerful or weak people—the top and the bottom (almost completely the bottom), letting the middle live on in ignorance, for the most part. Maybe that was just the media's portrayal, though, he decided, and he concluded that the United States was not so different from most countries that tried to control their images, both at home and abroad. Tobias would be considered high in society, portrayed by the media as an ivory tower lord. Amy as the queen. *Amy and the Hit Man*. It sounded like a punk rock group. Like night moths around a porch light, Digger's thoughts flapped and fell, some sizzling away, some sticking with a powdery, ghostly grip.

Along floor three of the Faculty Offices Building, the most famous floor in Ocean View College history, Digger had many short, uneasy conversations about Tobias, most focused on suspects (nobody mentioning Amy, though), the abrupt, unified conclusions being that a madman had struck and was long gone. While Digger did not argue, his thoughts whirled about whenever he was alone in his office, and none of them landed on a madman, unless it was Bill Jacobs. With December's arrival, Digger's colleagues all seemed flighty, too; nobody wanted to stay in his or her office. The Humanities corridor, ironically, was fuller of life than at any other time in Digger's memory, and not all the loiterers were English teachers. Everyone—teachers, staff, students—wanted to experience the scene of the crime, the knifing of Tobias Mann. The third floor reminded Digger of a cocktail party without any alcohol because the conversations were clipped and superficial.

"You have a nice view of the ocean from this building."

"Yes, you should see it on a sunny day."

"Where did it happen?"

"Down there."

Although his peers were somewhat introverted people, they all seemed to crave sociability and a strange celebrity now, standing about in the hallway with colleagues and strangers, sometimes just in silence, which always became personified when people were present. *Niggling* was the word that came to Digger's mind—a niggling silence.

At home, Simba pushed emptiness to the corners, so Digger brought her to school every day now, not just on the two class-less ones—Tuesday and Thursday—and her grinning presence assisted everyone. The Humanities Department needed some levity, and students, staff, and professors alike congregated around him and Simba, stroking her short tan hair and asking questions. Everyone loved the name Simba and told her what a beautiful girl she was. Simba had that aura. Around her, people talked to her, not to her human. When in class (Monday/Wednesday/Friday schedule), Digger often left Simba locked in his office, where she curled up beneath his desk and slumbered; however, sometimes for those two-hour stretches, he deposited Simba with a grateful Jessica Williams, who still appeared haunted and jumpy—except around the dog.

"Oh, you're so beautiful and smart!" Jess would coo directly into Simba's grinning face, and Digger reveled in the attention his dog earned. *Probably how people think about their kids.* He concluded that he was living through a dog now, and he didn't mind the summation.

The first week of December passed, and doors down the Humanities corridor began to close again. The crowds trickled away. When peers passed, talk turned from the unifying topic of Tobias Mann to the weather, the semester's end, problems with students. Halfway through the week, the administrators anointed the bearded Don Domberg as Acting Chair. Everyone got an email about it. Then they got another: Tobias Mann's funeral would take place on Saturday.

Digger went alone; after all, he could not take Simba to the funeral, although he did give it some thought. Simba was definitely a therapy dog even if nobody but Digger and Jessica Williams knew it. The Humanities Department represented itself well: Digger witnessed everybody but Bill Jacobs, but maybe Bill was seated closer to the front, to the casket. Although the Catholic church was especially spacious, stony and foreboding, all of the pews were filled starting halfway down the line, so Digger found space around the middle, in a pew with the unlikely pair of Elena Bonner and Paul Smith. *Like the singles table at a wedding*, thought Digger, but then he remembered that Paul did have a wife, that his wife had stayed. Elena, sporting a new Dutch-boy haircut, said hello and seemed genuinely glad to see him, and Paul nodded, his look sepulchral. Thinking that the funeral should be for Paul, Digger glanced over the crowd. No Dan the Religious Man; maybe he was a Protestant. "Where's Bill?" Digger said to Elena, but she didn't know. She had bangs now (sort of a Cleopatra look), and they swayed about a bit when she tilted her head. Her hair was dark brown and straight, and while Digger wanted to reach out and touch the swaying locks, he realized that he never would, that he was broken in all the right places.

"He's probably scared to enter a church," said Paul Smith without smiling, but Digger did. Elena leaned over and said, "Apparently, he's got nothing to fear since we're in here." Digger laughed softly, but Paul just turned away. Digger detected a stale odor and attributed it to all the wool coats steaming in the cold, lofty church.

Down in the pews, nobody else appeared to be smiling or even talking, just waiting in big stony silence. Digger looked at the backs of heads and saw one face, Omar Johns'. The administrator seemed to be searching for someone, but his gaze landed on nobody, just flashed by a couple of times. Digger had never seen a skinny man with a rounder head than Omar Johns, and Digger wondered if the administrator had been picked on as a kid, called Lollypop maybe, or Stick Head. *What's that lollypop with the chewy middle?* Maybe Omar Johns was called that as a kid. Maybe that was why his smile always seemed false, too quick and sickly sweet. Digger thought of funeral directors and politicians. Then of his father, of the Congregational church where his funeral had taken place—more wood and windows than this great stone room— and then of his sister, Emma, of the same Protestant church, warmer but similar to this one, both of them open and upward, directing the parishioner's gaze toward Heaven. On both occasions, Digger had looked out the clear Congregational windows at leaf-less trees, grey-brown and skeletal, and he realized now that he had never been to a funeral when the trees were decked out in seasonal glory. Turning toward the windows in this Catholic church, Digger saw just the attractive stained glass, tall and thin in every window, so he raised his gaze further, up the stiff, steep sides of the church. To Digger, though, the ceiling looked empty, just another blocked window. *Empty.* His mind shifted back to his sister. Emma had been divorced, too, and she had given his parents no grandkids, same as Digger, who wondered whether his mother felt any resentment about that fact, about their line ending—*most likely, anyway.* Before a child could appear, Digger would have to have a date. That thought made him laugh sadly, a little bitterly, but he kept these musings to himself.

"Where's Simba?" whispered Elena, and she smiled again (most did when Digger's dog was the focus).

"Believe me, I thought hard about bringing her. I've been taking her everywhere. But I've never seen a dog in a church, although I haven't seen all that many churches."

"You're a real heathen," Elena laughed quietly, her bangs swishing. "And if Simba doesn't belong in a church, then none of us do. That dog has saved Jessica. Without Simba last week, Jessica would have gone on vacation or even quit. As it is, she leaves early every day."

"She saved me," responded Digger, and they both knew that he meant Simba, not Jessica Williams. "Is Jess here?"

"Right over there near Don and his wife. That's Jessica's husband. I met him one day when he picked her up. Something to do with a broken-down car. He seemed like a nice guy. He didn't say much."

"Your bangs are swishing around," whispered Digger. "They look nice." Maybe Elena was part of what his mother meant about youth, part of the wave of youth.

"They cut it too short," she responded in a low tone, as though a whole team had wacked away at her head. Then she added quietly, "I never go to the hairdressers."

At that point, Paul Smith leaned over and said loudly, "It's too short. Women should have long hair."

"Is your wife's hair long?" whispered Elena, unperturbed, and Digger thought, *what's Paul's wife's name?* He couldn't remember. Paul didn't answer. Elena turned to wave at someone up ahead, and Digger spotted a psychology professor waving back. Digger waved, too, and then felt foolish since he didn't know the professor well and because Digger was obviously not the man's target. The swishing bangs were the target. Digger pondered the man's name—*Watkins?* He had seen campus-wide emails from the man, and he remembered his first name now, William. *William Watkins.* Digger shivered under a brush of jealousy, of loss, so he settled his gaze ahead at nothing, at the back of a head. *Everyone has brown hair*, he concluded.

Everyone stayed quiet now, glancing up and down, at the Bibles in the racks attached to the pews' backs, at the stained-glass windows, casting their multi-colored glow throughout the huge open room, at the backs of heads, at past problems and future successes, and especially at the open casket up near the pedestal where the priest would talk. From this distance, Tobias looked very good. Digger searched for the back of Amy's head and found it in a front-row pew. Her hair was not brown, it was blond, sort of, that old-lady blond that threatened to break out in primary colors in spots—a rising, layered hairstyle as though she had just walked out of the 1950's. A middle-aged guy was sitting next to her, and Digger thought of the hit man, that Amy had actually brought the killer to her husband's funeral. Then he realized that the man must be Tobias' son, Rick if he remembered right. Then it occurred to Digger that the son and the hit man could be the same, but then the service began. All thoughts drifted back to the deceased.

The only really memorable part, Digger thought afterwards, was that nobody cried. Rick got up and told a story about Tobias, how he had always supported his son, and one of Tobias' nephews or cousins or some neighbor's kid read a poem about death and it not being the end, but rather a sort of glorious starting line. *And he's off,* Digger felt warm and sleepy and tired. He glanced repeatedly at the widow. Amy didn't get up to speak or even move her head, except when Rick sat down after his say. For some reason, Digger wanted to see her expression. He thought of Tobias' will. After the poem, Jess looked as though she would cry, but then the priest read some more Bible passages, the congregation rose and sat, kneeled and sang, *the way Catholics do,* and after what seemed like way too long, the priest invited mourners to say goodbye to Tobias. The people in the front got to go first, so the back-pew people stood up again, waited in the aisle, sorted out the order, and then tottered down the middle path to kneel before Tobias. Digger's turn came soon enough, and he knelt along with custom and looked searchingly at Tobias's still face. The undertaker had done a fine job. Tobias appeared almost alive and very peaceful. Maybe his face was a little bloated, his skin a little too colored, and Tobias never looked peaceful before. Digger couldn't help but remember that the figure before him had been stabbed to death. In his mind, he told what was left of his colleague that he was sorry, and then Digger returned to his pew down the side aisle. Almost everyone went up and knelt down before the dead man. It took a long time. Digger wished that Simba were there, adding life and connection. In his mind, he could feel her soft, pointy ears, could hear her gentle "woof."

As the rear rows said good bye to Tobias Mann, Digger looked around at all the people, but could not find Bill or any police presence. Didn't the TV cops always attend the victim's funeral? *Most likely, Tobias' killer sat in one of these pews,* thought Digger uneasily. His mouth was dry, a stale coffee taste. He imagined a blue and silver Bud Light in his refrigerator. He would like to wash away this whole atmosphere. Digger remembered again his mother's pronouncement about everyone's getting younger. *Not in this church*, he concluded, except possibly Elena.

After everyone had had his or her turn, the priest read some more, yet Digger did not really pay attention. He felt even more sleepy. "I need a cup of coffee," he whispered to Elena, and she nodded in agreement, her bangs flopping a bit. The service ended somewhat abruptly, and Tobias' casket was wheeled past, amidst the swaying of incense and ringing of little bells, all calling the spirits to attend to a man's passage. Then the living all filed out to join the funeral line behind Tobias' hearse. Thinking of William Watkins, Digger asked Elena and Paul, who formed a little trio, if they wanted to ride with him. Paul nodded no (just one nod), but Elena accepted.

The trip to the cemetery took twenty minutes or so, due to the procession's slow pace, and Digger and Elena talked mainly of the service and the people there. However, a couple minutes from the graveyard, she did drop a bombshell of sorts.

"I shouldn't speak ill of the dead, but Tobias made a pass at me once."

"What!"

"A couple years ago, in his office, he made a pass at me. I had been requesting a Tuesday/Thursday schedule because of my community college courses. They were all on the Monday/Wednesday/Friday schedule. I told him I'd be grateful for Tuesday/Thursday classes, and he said 'How grateful?'"

"What did you say? I can't believe he would say that, the cad!"

"I just stammered a bit, mentioning the days of the week, and he said something like 'I certainly want to keep my adjuncts happy.' It was creepy. I never went to his office again. All email after that."

"I can understand that."

She had never told anyone about the incident and said that she wasn't sure why she was doing so now. Digger suggested sarcastically that she had been influenced by the big, stony church, that she was confessing, and Elena said seriously, "Maybe so." The episode with Mann had never been repeated, but it made Digger wonder about the other female staff, about Jess Williams, who'd been with OVC the longest. What stories might she have?

Elena's tale caused Digger unpleasant thoughts as the cemetery winds played about with everyone's hair, not just Elena's. He looked at the casket differently, pictured Tobias' rising out of it like Nosferatu. Then the sun slipped from behind a cloud, and Digger's thoughts changed. On the pleasant little hillside, Tobias' plot awaited him, the opening covered by a maroon tarp. No dirt showed, just the rectangular hole inversely wrapped by the satin-smooth tarp. "Nice," said Digger because it was nice: a somewhat sunny but cool early December day on a New England hillside beneath various types of trees and among grey and white tombstones. Then another cloud passed, dragging a shadow over the scene, and Digger's mood shifted again. He pictured Bill and Paul on either side of the hole, tall and stooped like a pair of gargoyles or giant vultures.

Digger turned away from the plot. The churchgoers had thinned, and William Watkins seemed to be one of those absent. Elena broke the silence.

"Last weekend I attended a funeral, my aunt's."

"Were you close to her?"

"Not really."

"Was she old?"

"Not really." Elena laughed at this repetition.

Digger chuckled, too, but felt a little stab of guilt that he had not known about Elena's personal life. He realized that until today he hadn't really talked to Elena all semester, maybe for a year now. Once he had wanted to ask her out, but after he had not acted on that impulse, the desire had faded, flickered out. Now, though, standing beside her, the early-winter breezes playing with her soft bangs, the memory of her confession fresh in his mind, Digger felt attracted to her. He glanced down at her new hairdo and wondered who was taller, Elena or Detective Doyle, but he pictured the little detective for just a few seconds because Elena's profile looked quite sweet indeed. What about William Watkins, that wave? *Innocent enough*, Digger decided, vowing to ask Elena out soon, no doubt about it, but now the priest was reading again, the familiar "valley of death" passage. Digger steeled himself for a long stand, yet the priest soon finished, as though he had another appointment, maybe another funeral. Then the holy man, black frocked, multi-layered, thanked everyone for attending and invited them back to the church for refreshments "in the rec room."

"That was nice," said Digger.

"It was," Elena agreed.

"The weather couldn't have been better," said Digger.

"The weather has been dry all semester," Elena replied.

"Yes," said Digger even though he remembered some recent snowfall.

As they left, people nodded to each other, and if they said anything at all, the mourners merely mirrored Digger and Elena's nice remarks.

With each step in the funeral process, more people disappeared, for the funeral seemed fairly packed, the burial less crowded, the reception somewhat sparse. The remaining Humanities people mostly sat together and talked about Tobias. Everyone agreed that he was a good chairperson; no one explained why. Very few stories were told, and the two or three offered anecdotes were pretty bland. Digger volunteered no tales. Paul Smith had appeared again, but he sat quietly, perhaps thinking about going home to his long-haired wife. Then Bill Jacobs arrived in time for some memorial cake. "What did I miss?" he said to Digger, as though this were all a department meeting. Digger was still feeling sleepy and silly, too, so he responded, "We all think the butler did it."

Bill Jacobs appeared about as un-butlery as a person could look; he seemed to have been doing some gardening. Digger noticed leaf pieces or crumbs in Bill's beard, but still he sort of liked the man. "You've got to watch out for those butlers," said Bill Jacobs, and Digger laughed a little. The others around the table stared at him. *Digger and the part-timers*, he thought, and then *Amy and the Hit Man*.

"Where's Gemma?" said Digger because Bill's wife had that odd name (Bill swore that it was her real name, too— "Right on the birth certificate"), and Bill shook his bearded head sadly. "Sick," he said. "I can't stay long. I have to bring her back some crackers."

Digger said that he hoped Gemma didn't have what was going around campus, that "half my students missed class yesterday, and the other half were all sniffling." Elena smiled at that and nodded her agreement: "Mine, too." Paul just looked down at his hands, reminding Digger of his students' clandestine efforts to hide their cell phones in their laps.

Bill made a scoffing sound. "You mean Affluenza," he leered. "No chance Gem or I will catch that OVC malady!"

As Digger and Elena started to chuckle (OVC's students tended to be well off, affluent), Paul Smith made an announcement, a handful of quickly mumbled words that sounded like "All wives seem to be ill or missing." Nobody responded to that, Digger brooding momentarily at the obvious reference to Anna. Soon after, Digger anticipated the party's breakup, and within two minutes, he saw Don Domberg at an adjoining table glance at his watch, then at his wife, then at the exit door. The new chairperson started a Humanities Department stampede of sorts, until just Digger and Elena sat sipping their third coffees and nibbling on seconds of pastries. Bill Jacobs had said "crackers" as he left, but Paul Smith had just faded off.

Digger leaned over to Elena and whispered, "If Tobias was a bit of a cad, like he was with you, wouldn't his wife have known about it? Could Amy have done it?"

This question caused Elena's new bangs to bounce about, and she whispered back, "You can't ask that here!"

Elena had nice eyes and lively hair, and Digger felt a warm apathy, sort of empty and reckless. "I'm whispering," he said in words that rose above a whisper. Then he smiled and did whisper again: "Amy might have done it. Wives can be pretty demanding. Wives can be cruel, merciless."

Elena knew Digger's history; everybody did, but she just shook her head and bangs. "Digger," she said quietly, even though nobody remained within a table of theirs, "No woman stuck a knife into Tobias, especially not Amy. She's not capable. She doesn't even do her own gardening." That was news to Digger, who thought of gardeners, potential hit men, a stuck knife, some kind of sharp garden tool. Elena broke back into his revelries: "Amy's actually a nice person. I liked her a lot more than her husband. And, Digger, I have to go, too. I've got papers that should have been returned before Thanksgiving!"

Digger didn't want her to leave, so he asked, "How was your aunt's reception?" He wasn't sure if that were the correct word.

"She wasn't getting married or bar-mitzvahed," laughed the young woman. "The Protestant church didn't host a gathering afterwards. We just all went back to my aunt's house, and everybody brought food—pot luck. I brought a pasta dish, as did a couple of my relatives. I don't remember eating much, but I have some cousins that tucked right in!" She laughed again, and so did Digger.

"These Catholics know how to make a strong cup of coffee. Good pastries, too, but I took a pass on those cheese and crackers."

"Worried about the Body of Christ, are you, Digger?"

"That's a good question. Nobody's ever asked me that." Digger was reluctant to let Elena Bonner go. He thought about the waving Psych teacher. Could she be seeing him? He wanted to ask but didn't. How could anyone date a psychology professor? If they were quiet, you would know that they were sizing you up, and if they were speaking, then they would be sizing you up. He said none of this, felt Elena's desire to leave, saw her eyes shifting to the door, and thought of Simba, whose gaze revealed her consciousness, her direction.

"Maybe we should become Catholics," he finally said.

"For the coffee? That seems a little extreme. What religion are you, anyway, Digger?"

"Raised a Congregationalist, but now ... I believe in Simba, in the birds flying about, in branches swaying. I guess I'm a pagan."

"Do you dance around a fire deep in the woods?"

"Not that I can remember." Digger laughed at that image.

"Then you're not a pagan," Elena concluded, and Digger thought of his mother, of the world's regression to youth. Elena had more answers than he did, so maybe he was in fact part of that youth movement.

"Digger, I have to go," Elena stated, and she got right up. "I enjoyed the company. Much more entertaining than my cousins."

Digger smiled, said that he was "just going to sit here a bit longer." He didn't add that he enjoyed her company, too, but he almost said it.

Digger watched Elena go, liked the way she looked, and wondered again why his desire to pursue her had burned out, as well as why the little flame seemed to have self-lighted. Fear? Apathy? Now jealousy? He had lived with jealousy for so long that he hardly recognized its prickling fire anymore. Anna had been the love of his life (if not he hers), but did that mean he had to be alone? He was like a faithless monk, saved from insanity and despair by a dog, a little piece of lighted Heaven. Maybe that was all there was for us humans, little pieces of Heaven, tiny lights. Alone at the table, Digger sipped lukewarm coffee and felt Mann's family and friends pass him by in small groups on their way to the exit.

Chapter Ten: Imagery

When writing a college essay, don't get caught up creating imagery—i.e., using superfluous adjectives and similes. For the most part, except maybe to start and end the paper, mental pictures do little to support a composition's purpose since most academic writing involves explanation, not description. Professors want to know what you know, what you think, so if you dazzle them with imagery, they will think mainly that you don't follow directions.

Digger poured the Bud Light from its blue and silver can into a glass beer mug because he liked to watch the golden color and the swirling white bubbles, enjoyed seeing the beer rise as the foam popped, and then take a slow swig when the bubbles left just a layer of frosting atop the mug. Simba raised her head toward him and stared without reproach, and Digger said, "You want some beer, Simba? A little's not bad for you." He tilted a thin layer into a bowl and placed it before the dog, who happily and noisily lapped it up. Digger drank again, somewhere between a sip and a swig, and then looked out the kitchen window at the coming of the day's end. Two chickadees were getting their last meal of the day. They zipped to his feeder, grabbed a seed, and popped back to a blue-spruce branch to crack their feast. Then they repeated the procedure. They journeyed through their simple lives in pairs, same with the cardinals. Watching the efforts of the little black and white birds, along with the backdrop of crawling waves and slowly marching white clouds (going grey), Digger experienced how wondrous life could be, a thought that rose often when he stood at this window, watching nature, or when he stared into Simba's dark eyes and saw the light shining up from deep inside, the little star in those marble-black depths.

How wondrous! That thought exploded at the end of the first Bud Light, danced about during the second, became fuzzy and enlarged by the end of the third, and started to transform into mere contentedness and then sadness somewhere during the fourth, disappeared completely after that. Before long, Digger reached *after that* even though the sun still hung above the ocean, brushing both sea and sky with a kaleidoscope of colors, twinkling the wave tops, refusing to give way to night.

Years ago, when he and Anna had first moved into the cottage, Digger would throw bread to the backyard birds, but the gulls ended that idea. Out of thin air, the seagulls came, descended, and devoured, dozens of them, hundreds. Like a bad horror movie, even worse with all the white globs of gull poop left after the frenzy. The same craziness happened when Digger took an old loaf out to the beach. The nearby gulls scuttled after him like great feathered crabs, while the buoyed ones in the sea rose up and hovered about him, wafting and waiting and wanting, and even the specks of gulls far away would come tearing through the air, growing almost instantly. Afterwards, Anna had said that for a moment she thought the seagulls would carry Digger away. He had laughed. He had thought so, too. Maybe that would have been better.

After Anna had left him, Digger bought the spindly blue spruce (an accent tree), the bird feeder tube, the pole, and forty pounds of sunflower seeds. He needed some life in the cottage, and the birds lit that doused little flame in him. They seemed to sew the heavens to the earth, and he needed some connection, some repair. Almost two years later, Digger went to the Ocean View Pound and walked up and down the aisles, petting the dogs that pushed themselves into the bars of their cages, stopping twice in front of a curled up hound that looked at him but didn't rise. Something about that black-muzzled and inward animal spoke to Digger, so he took her for a walk and fell in love. "You look like a little lion," he'd told the little spirit that walked sedately but steadily at his side. "I'm going to call you Simba. Do you like that? Simba?" When he walked her from the pound, Simba grew more energetic, and when he let her out the pickup door in his driveway, the rescued dog leaped like a dolphin, making Digger wonder what he'd gotten himself into. But Simba soon proved to have that perfect amount of doggy energy and peace, bringing laughter, lightness, and some tangible meaning back to Digger's life.

Light and warmth—Simba brought both to the cottage, but the rooms were still so quiet. In warm weather and sometimes even cold, Digger would open the kitchen window to hear the pounding growl and swish of the sea (the bay, really), the crazed dinosaur yearning of the gulls, the sweet chickadee-dee-dee of the black-capped song birds, the single cheep of the cardinals' sudden appearance. Those were all nice sounds, even the seagull screams, but at times the wild just accented the quiet. Sometimes Digger would walk from one little room to another and think, "Am I dead?" Then he would turn and see Simba, his shadow of light, his warm trailing cloak, and she would be looking expectantly up at him, sparkling and questioning, her head cocked to one side, her mouth dropping open in a grin, her tail journeying back and forth, back and forth. Digger would bend down and say "What? What is it, Simba?" And she would respond with "woof," low and guttural, a whisper from the wild, from the bright side of dark existence, a connecting call. Digger would laugh then and feel at home.

Alone but for Simba and a line of empty, dented beer cans, Digger laughed no more on this day turning into night. Laughter had been engulfed by dusk. Perhaps he would scoff at some television show or maybe more inwardly at some fragmented memory—Anna's laughter or just a smile, a kind remark, hands held—but the sound would carry no mirth, no wonder at life's beauty. At these times, even Simba disappeared from Digger's consciousness, for he wandered so far down the past's shadowed pathways that Digger became lost within himself, within the darkness, in the river that never stopped and that always rolled by beneath cover of consciousness.

Down the path from the south end of campus, about two miles down from Digger's cottage, OVC ended at the sea in a rocky little beach favored by beer-drinking students and seagulls. Standing halfway up the hill, the hooded presence heard the birds now: EEaaayuht, Eahyut, Eahyut, Eahyutyutyutyutyut... The gulls soared and screamed, a sound less of feathers and air than of scales and skin, flecks of blood. Listening, the figure crept down the path, following the two students, the boy and girl. Hearing the screams of the gulls, understanding their lament to days past, then slipping behind a tree, an indention in the hillside, some scrub bush, he (she?) stalked the pair.

About pronouns, Digger would advise his students to avoid agreement errors by using plural nouns, such as "people" or "readers," instead of wordy "he or she" phrasing, but Digger wasn't at this scene, was he? Two chickadees were, perhaps the pair from Digger's own backyard, zipping home to some sheltered branch. Noting the furtive human below, they announced their name to the wild, a warning, and kept their little black-capped heads cocked, an eye each down at what looked like a typical two-foot giant but acted like a four-footer. The day's end bid them haste—to home and harbor.

Night was falling quickly now, and the two young people increasingly sensed only themselves and their narrowed consciousness. Too far away to hear their sophomoric speech, the hooded figure reveled in the gull's auditory dives, a descent into madness and then back to the freedom of height, and the figure recognized the rise and fall. This human understood what all the rest would consider madness, *but what do they know?* They knew nothing of other people's lives, of such descents, such rising. They thought only of their own concerns, so the other would give them more. Provide retribution. *Let Mann's wife hide in her castle. At OVC, the hiding's good, too. And the hunting.* The hooded figure watched the boy and girl stroll away down the beach. Following them would be easy, a simple matter of choice. With night dropping like a shroud, the waves lunging and lapping, the two fools were oblivious, lost in love. Again, a gull passed with a honking scream, the sound beneath a flat and heavy stone pried open with a crowbar.

Outside Digger's cottage, the song birds had disappeared, even the cardinals, the last avian visitors of the day, their single cheeps swallowed by the shadowed hood of night. The bay had become a dark sheet rippled with white lace. One gull called, muffled and distant, like a childhood memory. Even Simba was asleep, laid out on the couch like a folded comforter. Two miles down toward the open mouth of the Atlantic, the boy and girl had returned to the path leading up to the college. Together, they were alone, the shadows to left and right containing only emptiness.

"Simba!" Digger sent the word out to search the darkness, to gain some light, but she did not respond. Traveling through the images of her own dreams, the lion dog slept deeply. Digger, too, would not remember this night.

Chapter Eleven: Comparisons

Comparisons not only provide effective evidence, but also lead directly to understanding concepts and retaining knowledge. The best teachers are examples, actual models, and by comparing writing (professional texts and novice ones, such as their own efforts), students will see a wide range of illustrations, from great to woeful, each beneficial to the learning process.

As an English teacher, Digger was of course a great reader. Even before Anna had left, he'd spent many nights cradling a book, and sometimes she would join him. Digger remembered that soft scene within a little cone of light, the darkness beyond the windows, the sheltering peace and comfort, the almost complete absence of sound. When he pictured those snapshots, less and less with time's passage, Digger could not understand his former wife, her unrest, her abandonment. Since her leaving, he read even more, revisiting many books, old friends, especially the mysteries of Hillerman and Mankell because those authors created characters from the stark landscapes themselves, the western deserts and Sweden's southern coast. The main characters, too, felt comfortable to Digger, partly because the fictional heroes lived alone, worked hard to exist in an empty world. Everyone needed camaraderie even if it came from just fictional beings. In those western and Swedish worlds, too, the winds were always howling, and Digger could relate to that sound, could hear it whenever he opened a window and imagined it even when his cottage's openings were all closed. In Hillerman's and Mankell's worlds, the horizons were big, the humans small, and Digger saw that, too, when he looked at the surging bay or at the Atlantic from many windows at OVC.

When he read now, he sometimes recited passages to Simba. She paid attention, her pointed ears rotating, her big head cocking left, then right, and then Simba nestled that beautiful noggin into her short front paws to be bathed in all the words, the bubbling flow of language. Soon, with December's progress, Digger would be able to read even more.

The last week of classes arrived, bringing a few more flurries but no buildup of snow, just chilly, cloudy days that whispered *winter*, along with the first version of Digger's students' final papers. In his George North class, Digger wrote three words high on the board: *Positive Peer Review*. When he turned to face the class, his eyes fell on the back row, to the left, to George and his two apathetic apostles. For the past two weeks, George had risen up to be a leader, and though normally that fact would have brightened Digger's day, it instead bothered him because George's leadership always offered an edge, subtly sarcastic and cutting. The three back-row boobs stared back at Digger, seemingly awaiting his orders yet grinning a bit, *like hyenas*, thought Digger, glad that he had decided to form groups himself for this activity. The three hyenas would not plot together today, he vowed, but then another thought beckoned: *Hyenas kill in packs, not alone—don't they?*

This afternoon's 102 class had sixteen students, almost all good at attending, so Digger used the roster and created four sections on the board, four students to a section, the three boobs in different groups, a fourth boob—another hyena who had not found the pack—in the final quartet. Having learned all of his students' names within the semester's first three weeks, Digger wrote the correct four names above each quarter of the board. "Group One here," he said, pointing to the names and then to the first row right side. "Bring all your stuff to your group and dial up your final projects. Group Two here." With no problems and good speed, Digger arranged the four groups. The students all started their laptops, a couple using cell phones, and accessed the files to their final 102 paper.

Then Digger explained the Positive Peer Review activity and the reasons for this comparative exercise: "First, you compare elements from your own papers in your groups, finding the 'best' example. Then you compare the examples on the board, analyzing the 'best' of those. Each 'best' overall earns its group five free minutes, and if two groups tie, then I divide up the minutes. Nobody loses here. The free minutes are great, but what really matters is that you understand the compared examples and then apply that knowledge to your own papers. To improve your skills, you need more knowledge. Knowledge and practice—that's what leads to skills acquisition." Then Digger concluded his little speech by giving the class his judgment criteria for the "best": clear and specific—"The keys to great college essays."

"Ready?" asked Digger. "Everybody's paper out? The first content element to compare is your essay's title. Share those titles, debate whose is best, and put it on the board under your names. Five free minutes up for grabs!"

Understandably, Digger's students liked free minutes. In his own college experiences, Digger didn't remember moving much. On the first day of every class, he would find a chair (around the third row, usually) and then stick to it for the next three and a half months, staring forward the whole class, unless he looked sideways or backwards at a student who decided to join in the "class" discussion. His professors had never offered free minutes, and a teacher would let students out early only when he or she (usually he) ran out of material. That was rare. In his past, the professors were the stars, a few talkative students the moons, and the rest of them (usually including him) just dark matter. Digger didn't decide on a teaching career in order to repeat those sins; he wanted his students to be the stars, for them to teach each other, for him to step back and manage the activity, more like a coach, in fact. This philosophy had worked for Digger for all his years at OVC and even during graduate-school teaching. Without it (and the mostly positive student evaluations his lessons led to), Digger knew that he would not have earned a full-time position, or more importantly even enjoy his job.

Two groups sent their emissaries to the board, then three, and then the fourth, George North's group. George launched himself up. On the whiteboard, the ink pens made their little squeaking, and then the writers drifted back to their groups, George with an unnerving grin on his puss. Digger would review that title last; it waited to the far right of the board anyway. To himself, Digger read the four finalists, the titles for the last paper, a self-analysis of the students' current writing capabilities and improvements:

1. Project Four: My Improvements
2. How My Writing Has Improved
3. Bad, Better, Best
4. What I Learned from Two Men; One Alive and One Dead

It was happening again, thought Digger in horror: George North was mocking Tobias—*and mocking me* ... Yet that title wasn't bad, and Digger supposed that it didn't really mock Tobias at all, *did it?*

"Remember my criteria," Digger finally decreed. "While I like one of these titles, it isn't clear enough. Can you see which?" As usual, with comparative exercises like these, students could be led to the answer (rather than just given it), and a handful of them pointed to the third column on the board: *Bad, Better, Best.* That had been the name of one of Digger's handouts, three model paragraphs that illustrated the second paper assignment, a linguistic analysis. One body paragraph (Bad) had been completely off topic, despite offering a deceptively clear topic sentence; another had provided "A" quality analysis, showing especially specific reasoning; and the third model had been "Better" but somewhat skimpy in its explanations, which needed unity, too.

About the group's use of this title, Digger said, "Right," adding "What is Bad, Better, and Best? I like that idea, but it just isn't clear enough, doesn't preview the paper's purpose. Nice try, though, and with some revision, that idea could work well."

Then Digger studied the board again, turned, and said, "Two other titles aren't specific enough—which two?" As always (almost), the compared examples provided the answers for the students themselves. With shaking heads of sad comprehension (in the first two groups) and wide smiles (George's group), the class acknowledged that the reference to two teachers made the fourth group's title specific while the word "learned" pointed clearly to the paper's purpose.

"I really like this plan," pushed Digger. "Elements learned in this class and in Professor Mann's—I presume—101 class." Digger decided not to share his worries over the title's possible sarcasm, but he could see little lights in his students' eyes—just mischievous, though, not malevolent. Even though it bugged him to give George's group five full minutes, he had to. That title clearly won.

"Okay, what's next?" he continued, trying to move his students along because this exercise took time and he wanted to get as many examples on the board as possible. "Your main focuses, your thesis. Find yours and share it with the group. Whose thesis is the clearest and most specific? Get your 'best' thesis on the board as soon as possible."

Again the groups clustered, a sight that Digger enjoyed, that made him feel positioned correctly in this world, and before long, one student detached from each team and added the group's example to the board. George had gone first this time (the same students usually wrote each time although some groups alternated), and Digger read the unraveling thesis: "Through these two professors, I improved in three main areas." *Wow*, thought Digger because that was another winner, and he realized that he could get rid of George North earlier than usual today if nobody else's thesis were that strong. And George's group did win all five minutes again, as all the other groups acknowledged, reluctantly, that the fourth group's thesis was more specific due to the "three main areas" point, a reference left out of the other three theses, which all pointed to improvements, but not to a number. Digger praised all the theses and revised his five-minute reward by giving the other three quartets one minute apiece and George's group five. Everybody was happy.

"What goes up next?" said Digger, and one student suggested "topic sentence." "Soon," he replied, "but what I want to see next is your essay's very first sentence, your introduction's first sentence. Compare and share." The students passed around laptops, traded phones, and talked, but one student said to Digger (it was the pack-less hyena), "Do you mean the first sentence in our whole essay?" and Digger responded that he did mean just that. Eventually, the four best first sentences appeared on the board:

1. Wikipedia defines change as, "...a gradual progression due to time."
2. Change is all around us, in the weather, in the seasons, and in ourselves.
3. If my writing skills were an automobile they would be a '65 Mustang convertible due to all the revisions required and the shining results.
4. When I first walked into Professor Mann's 101 class last January, I looked at the old man and thought, "He won't live to see May."

Again, Digger was struck dumb, staring at the fourth entry, re-reading it to determine if it were great, inappropriate, what? He admitted to himself that the sentence was compelling and that he could not necessarily see mockery, that any student could have looked at Tobias and seen an old man.

But that reference to death unnerved him again, so he switched to the other entries, which he had first scanned as they emerged on the board. He really liked the car analogy one, especially the "shining results" wording because it related to the assignment without being too obvious and boring. Needed a comma, though, but that was okay. Digger liked the "seasons" sentence, too, the nice parallelism, and for a moment he felt sort of proud, but the Wikipedia one settled his lips again—*not a Wikipedia quote, with errors no less!* Not wanting to praise all but one group, Digger said, "These are all good. This story one about Professor Mann is compelling, and I really like analogies, especially with nice phrasing like 'shining results,' which could make for a nice essay title. I really like this parallelism, too, and the way it leads to 'ourselves,' to the writer. And definition often works well to start a paper. Just remember that no pause means no comma and that you don't need ellipses up front due to the lowercase first word. Anyway, these all work, so everybody gets two minutes." Applause broke out, Digger laughed at the enthusiastic noise, and on a sheet of notepaper, he kept track of the points: twelve now for George's group. With one more five-minute win, George would be gone for the day already.

"A jump ahead now," said Digger. "After comparing your first sentences, share your final ones, the last sentence in your conclusion. Who has the best one, right now? Share, compare, and put the best on the board."

Since all the students had now won points, each group seemed happy and talkative, collaborative, so Digger awaited the results feeling fine. He hoped that these final sentences would point back to the first ones, for that was a good essay tactic, one that he called "bookending." Bit by bit, the groups released a member, two groups choosing different writers this time. They displayed these "last" sentences:

1.   With the progression of time, I hope to change even more.
2.   Change is inevitable, and my writing changes have been for the better this semester.

3. My '65 Mustang will keep me cruising down the endless path of college essays.

4. So that's what I learned from two men, one alive and one dead.

Not bad, concluded Digger, more prepared for the final "final" sentence due to seeing that paper's title. "Two of these are more specific than the other two, but all work well. I'm going to give two two minutes and two one minute each. Which two are more specific?" Within half a minute, that question was answered, by the students themselves, and the third and fourth groups were awarded extra minutes. George's group had now earned 14 minutes, two short of the class' end, so Digger decided to let them go after starting the next idea.

"Up next," said Digger, "is any sentence with a quotation in it, any sentence from a body paragraph, with a quote, though." Then he approached George's group and whispered, "Very nice work. Clear and specific, and nice controlled ideas. I look forward to seeing all your papers. Any questions?" Faces grinned, and heads shook horizontally. "No," replied one student (not George). "I'm all set."

As Group Four broke apart, the individuals passed their teacher and said "thanks" and even "Merry Christmas," but George held back. When he strolled by Digger on his way to the door one last time, the student smiled, announced "It's been real," and shuffled out of Digger's life. Digger could think of no reply other than a negative one, so he just watched his receding student and pondered that odd word: *real.* He thought, too, about the vague word "it," probably his least favorite word (along with "is"). With that vague, confusing phrase, Digger realized that George North had just made an appropriate exit from his life.

Chapter Twelve: Coordination

The popular acronym for remembering coordination is fanboys*: for, and, nor, but, or, yet, so. These little words connect equal information, so avoid coordinating too much—i.e., making too many ideas stand out. Try scanning your essay for the word "but" and then checking to see if the idea after that contrasting word seems more important than the one before it (often the case). If so, simply add a subordinating word—such as "although," "while," or "whereas"—to the sentence's beginning and delete the coordinating "but." That way, you now stress the more important second idea because you have subordinated the less important first one. Coordination offers an important connecting tactic for equal ideas, but do not use it too often.*

On the last day of fall classes, a Thursday close to mid-December, accumulating snow fell across the Ocean View campus for the first time that winter. The school's president and two influential administrators, one being Omar Johns (Tobias Mann's least favorite official), volleyed back and forth via phone about cancelling classes, all three deciding not to do so. Therefore, some students plunged through the storm that late afternoon as Digger and Simba sat in his office, watching the pretty scene and listening to an occasional gull cry, ripping at the falling air. So far, no student had graced his Thursday office hours.

Done with his final class the day before, Digger felt happy, warm despite the cold scene beyond the window, peaceful despite the murder that still haunted everyone's sub-conscience, despite the killing having been drawn almost three weeks into history now. The Humanities corridor seemed emptied; even Jessica the secretary had gone home. But then, Digger heard a door open, the shuffle of feet and then papers, so he went out his door and down the hall to investigate, Simba shadowing him, of course. He stopped in the adjunct faculty office doorway, surprised, because he saw Bill Jacobs' back (due to his morning schedule, Bill rarely stayed at OVC beyond noon). After pausing but being unable to connect his thoughts into a statement or worthwhile question, Digger simply said, "Hi, Bill."

"Oh, it's you two, is it?" Bill Jacobs responded, pleasantly enough, and Simba ambled forward to a head rub. "This is a great dog," said Bill, and Digger responded that there was no better. As the men watched, Simba walked in a few tight circles, as though she were chasing her tail, and then selected a spot between them, laying her body down into a C shape.

Digger enjoyed Simba's getting comfortable and then looked up at his peer. "You're here late. All finished?"

Bill said, "Affirmative" and "Grading papers" and "What a load of," but instead of finishing that thought, the bearded man just smiled, best described by Digger as a "leer." Digger had always felt a little uneasy around Bill Jacobs, who seemed to plow through life at a bit of an angle, yet Digger had always felt connected to him, too, partly because they both began as adjuncts more than a dozen years ago. Digger remembered the shared adjunct office as almost a community center, unlike his own room, which often felt empty and deserted, like a closet. The adjunct office always had at least one person sitting inside, and Digger often used to venture in to relive old times with Bill, to hobnob with Elena, or to say hello to some newer adjunct (always a new one or two each fall semester). But each semester he made that venture less often, and the other full-timers never seemed to visit this office—too busy, too drawn to their own cubbyholes, their own importance? Maybe just too lazy. Bill would say that the full-timers were worried about catching Adjunctivitis (had he once said that?). At heart, though, Digger craved connection, even if just shallow touches, so he continued to join with the adjuncts now and again. With Bill, fifteen years had built a bond, albeit a weak one, forged on shared time and space.

"We haven't really talked about Tobias," said Bill, looking up from Simba, too. "About who killed him," and Digger realized that Bill's honesty was part of that tenuous connection between them, a line that seemed snapped for a couple of years after Digger was promoted to full-time status while Bill was left sharing an office with all the other adjuncts.

"Who do you think did it?" asked Digger, eager now because he hadn't had an in-depth conversation with anyone, really, except Detective Doyle. It was as though all the other inhabitants of this corridor feared to linger on the subject, the killer, as though not talking extensively about the murder somehow erased it a bit.

"My first thought was Dan the Man," offered Bill, surprising Digger since Dan always acted so complimentary toward Tobias. "You see," continued Bill, "Dan has a key to this building, and the killer must have had a key. The doors show no sign of break-in. I looked, and no doors or keys have been replaced. Tobias must have locked the door after him or been let in. Did Tobias have a key?"

Digger, now realizing that he was not the only amateur sleuth, replied that he'd never thought of a key (a fact that bothered him) and that Tobias must have had one. How else could he have entered the building on the Sunday of a holiday weekend? "I don't have a key," Digger admitted, thinking about others who might. "Who else has a key, besides Tobias and Dan?"

"Jessica Williams," said Bill in a knowing tone that cast suspicion on the secretary. "I get here around the same time as she does for eight AM classes, around 7:45, and I've seen her opening the outside door. I can't truthfully see her killing Tobias, though. She liked him, more than anyone else, anyway. She found him, you know (Digger said that he did know). She's too timid, too scared. She couldn't plunge a knife into a man's back." Bill gave that leer again, like a shadow creeping out, a shadow rimmed with teeth.

Was Tobias stabbed in the back? Did the papers mention that fact? Digger supposed that he must have been, snuck up on and then slaughtered. "Jess would have to be the greatest actress of all time," said Digger. "At Tobias' funeral, she was the only one who looked to be shedding tears, and every other time I see her, she still looks about ready to scream or cry."

"Nobody cried at Tobias' funeral?" mused Bill Jacobs. "I came late, you know. No real reason. Almost didn't go at all, but Gemma gave me a push, not one that included her, of course. What about Dan the Man? He must have been *lording* it up and getting religiously emotional."

"He wasn't there," revealed Digger. "I didn't see him, and I looked, probably in an effort to avoid him."

The leer appeared and one guffaw—mirth controlled. "Wrong denomination, I guess," Bill concluded, adding quickly, "He's my prime suspect, anyway. The guy's nuts, and only a nut would kill Tobias that way. Who's your prime suspect, by the way? Probably me!"

Digger noticed that Simba's eyes had been opening and shifting periodically from him to the leering man, deciding that his dog didn't quite trust Bill Jacobs. Then he decided that he did in fact trust this strange man. "No," he laughed, feeling just a little guilty. "You're too honest. If you'd killed Tobias, you'd have declared 'No Contest' and be in jail right now. I know that you and Tobias had some disagreements, but you wouldn't have killed him. Right?"

Now Bill Jacobs laughed, that leer stained to his face. "I wanted to kill him, but that was years ago, back when I still wanted to be full-time. Not now. I want to come and go quickly now. So I missed my murderous chance. I just don't care enough about it anymore."

Unsure about what to say to that, Digger realized that he should say something, request some explanation, but he instead said, "What about the other full-timers? Have you gone through the list?"

"I try not to think of them," said Bill Jacobs.

"They're not bad." Digger was also not sure how to explain that point, where to start. "They just have their own concerns, and their own little offices, plus a lot of meetings."

"I'm glad I avoided it." But Bill, head down, eyes averted, didn't look glad, thought Digger.

Digger shifted the focus. "I know that none of the full-time women did it. Can you imagine Mary or Catherine killing Tobias?"

Bill said that he could hardly imagine a "Mary" any more since nobody had that old-fashioned name these days: "I haven't had a student named Mary in twenty years." Digger said that he hadn't either even though he hadn't been teaching for quite that long.

Then Bill said "Catherine" in a sarcastic way, followed by, "Cathy couldn't do it, not unless Tobias called her Cathy." Digger laughed at that, and Simba looked up at him, her tail thumping the floor. Nobody would cut Catherine's name in half; from her upright expression, even strangers would see that her name was not to be shortened.

"What about that newer one, that Juliet?"

"Jolie," said Digger, adding, "She's gay," as though that fact eliminated her as a suspect.

"Maybe Tobias was a homophobe. Seemed like some kind of *phobe* to me."

"Women kill with poison," said Digger, even though he didn't know where that thought came from—TV probably. Digger realized that he was enjoying this coordinated investigation. Bill could be a negative conversationalist, but he could add some truths not seen at the usual angles. Digger tossed his peer another angle: "What about the men? Don, Eliot, Jeff, Bill, Todd. I don't know Todd that well, but the others don't strike me as murderers. They seem a little too wrapped up in themselves."

"Todd?" said Bill Jacobs, his lips twisted—a smile, a frown? "Who's that?"

"The new full-timer. He's been here for a couple years. He's from the Midwest."

"Don't know him from Adam," said Bill, but Digger suspected that he did, that he just didn't want to acknowledge a new full-timer, that he still harbored resentments at being passed over back when Digger was raised from the masses.

Digger added that Todd was a good guy and then changed the subject: "I sort of suspect a student. One that I have this semester and that Tobias had last spring. This guy's a real piece of work, sort of a blank exterior, but what's going on beneath it, huh?" Bill said that he suspected all his students, laughed at his own joke, and then requested some reasons, so Digger continued. "Nothing concrete, of course. He doesn't bring a bloody knife to class or anything, but he once had a run-in with Tobias, over grades, I think. Jess told me about it."

"Maybe she was trying to create a false trail." Both men laughed at that, and Simba glanced up from Digger to Bill and back to Digger, her ears rotating a couple times to catch the joke, her tail thumping the floor three times. Both Bill and Digger reached forward simultaneously to pat the dog.

"This student, I don't want to say his name, but he brings up Tobias in class, not in any nostalgic way either, more in a subtly mocking manner. He gets under my skin."

"Does he have any friends, any cohorts?"

"The bad ones always do," said Digger. "What's that saying? You can have one donkey, but if you have two, then beware because then they'll breed. Some college basketball coach said that about problem athletes."

Bill Jacobs laughed and leered again. "Now all the donkeys have cell phones," he scoffed, and Digger realized that his old colleague had smiled more times in the last ten minutes than Digger had seen in the last ten years. The mirth made Digger feel good, feel connected. Reveling in this coordinated analysis with his one-time prime suspect, Digger smiled but stayed quiet. Simba had lain her head back down and fallen asleep.

The day after Anna left, Digger had sat immobile on the sofa, listening to the growing silence, the way it started just out of the range of hearing and then became a head-filling sound, a one note piercing lament. Not an empty sound at all, more like a muffled scream originating deep within his own ears and punctuated by steady clicking—tsk, tsk, tsk, tsk, tsk, ... Digger had realized then that the kitchen clock had been plowing onward, digging at the emptiness in a sort of mocking and anxious way. That clock moved him, mentally and then physically. He had raised himself from the couch (it had taken some effort to rise), removed the plate-shaped clock from its screw in the kitchen wall (just over the sink), stumbled out to the backyard (not landscaped so prettily back then, more like a fenced in sand pit), and flopped on the back steps, halfway down. The clock had continued to hammer away with its double-A heart, and Digger watched the passing seconds. That day had been windy, stormy, and Digger felt the pull of those forces and heard the gulls' "eayut, yut, yutting" away on their edge of the world. Then he had swung the time piece in a concise arc right into the concrete left side of the steps, once (crack), twice (plastic flying), three times (disintegration and bloody knuckles). I've stopped time, Digger had thought to himself, plastic and little pieces of metal all about him, like feathers after a hawk's silent, stealthy kill.

He had left time broken in his backyard for a week, but then he put the remains in a bag, stabbing a finger on one jagged piece of plastic, not feeling much pain, though. A year or so later, he had bought another clock, a better one—made of walnut, metal works, and glass—a clock with the same plate shape but without a voice, a silent messenger of time. Digger told himself that he had upgraded, hanging the new time piece in the old spot, on the old screw. While the new clock looked nice and kept time to a tee, Digger had to try to like it. He had never really succeeded. Rarely checking the expensive clock (using the microwave's blue digital numbers, instead), Digger often thought of smashing it (around the five-beer mark, usually), of repeating his back-yard violence.

Into the comfortable silence created by donkeys and cell phones, a gust of wind clutched at the office window, a snow flurry dancing madly in the outside world. "What about me?" Digger, coming out of his reverie, said to Bill Jacobs. "Did you think that I killed Tobias?"

"What for?" said the other. "Tobias never hurt you, you got the job, and you have too strong of a guide" He bent and scuffled Simba's head again, waking her. "Now if your ex-wife had been murdered, I'd have thought of you immediately."

"I could never kill Anna," Digger said automatically, more to himself than to Bill. "I'm a clock smasher, not a people smasher." Bill leered at that strange reference but chose not to respond. Probably he was not interested in clocks; maybe he understood it somehow and imagined the carnage.

"Okay," said Digger, changing the subject as another wind gust assaulted the building, announcing that winter was not just coming, but here. As if in tandem, a gull rent the heavens like a dinosaur that had just spotted movement, a man in the brush. "We have Dan, although I don't think he did it, and Jess, who like Dan had a key. But she didn't do it either. You and I didn't do it. Why would any faculty member murder Tobias? What would they get from it, revenge? That's a motive just in the movies."

Bill cut in. "What about Paul? He's not the same guy anymore. He's been acting strange all semester, stranger than usual." And Digger thought, *the Stranger.*

"We're all a little strange," Digger admitted, adding with a small laugh "present company included."

"No argument there."

"The cops," began Digger, "they think that a stranger might have done the deed."

"You mean that little cop, Doyle?" smirked Bill. "I didn't know that cops could be that short. Don't they have height requirements? Probably not, now that diversity's the rage. The women would have to have height requirements, too. Equal opportunity for most."

Ignoring most of this brief rant, which veered a bit to the right, Digger latched onto the little detective's height deprivation: "Have you seen him standing?" For a moment, neither man focused on the murder. This new conversation felt oddly entertaining. Unfortunately, it petered out because Bill had never seen a standing Doyle, either, just a sitting one.

"Doyle thought that I did it," said Bill. "He interviewed me at the police station the day afterwards. He asked me one question after another and put all the answers into his computer. I could tell that he considered me a suspect. I told him about Pinsky and Jessica and the keys. I didn't want to be a suspect."

"I told him about you," admitted Digger, and the two men laughed again, a real honest release, coordinated in communication. Simba's tail thumped three times again, but her eyes stayed closed. Digger hadn't realized how heavy his confession to the little detective had made him feel. Within the echoes of their laughter, a phone called out—Digger's down the hall (too loud to be anyone else's behind those closed doors).

I'd better go answer that," said Digger, adding that he'd enjoyed talking and that Doyle considered him to be a suspect, too.

Bill leered, said, "To murder," and doffed an imaginary cap in farewell.

It was his mother calling. "I tried to reach you at home," said Jean Diggerson. "But since that dog of yours can't answer, I thought of the college."

"Simba's here with me now," replied Digger good-naturedly, and it was true: the tan hound with the short legs had ambled after him and now reclined behind his office chair. "What's up? Are you okay?"

Digger's mother admitted reluctantly that she was okay, just that she was old, and she told him her age again. Although he himself no longer felt exactly young (at forty-one, Digger had traveled just beyond the smooth frontal edge of middle age, but still remained a long distance from its jagged ending border), Digger paid little attention to years, to time, not after smashing it all those years ago. "I'm at school," he told his mother. "A friend, colleague, and I were trying to figure out who killed Professor Mann. We think it was his butler."

"That's morbid," judged Jean Diggerson. "How are you? When are you going to come visit me? I'm seventy-three, you know. I won't be here forever."

Digger doubted that last point, but he said instead, "Today's the last day of school. I have reams of essays to grade, and then I have to submit final grades. Christmas— that's when I'll see you, maybe Christmas Eve. I bought you two nice presents, so you'd better get me something nice— Simba, too."

Jean Diggerson added something like, "Oh, that dog," but Digger couldn't crack the tone and decided not to try. As she said something else, he thought about her comment about age and youth, the one that made no sense, so he cut into her words. "You mentioned that everybody's getting younger; what did you mean by that?"

After his mother said, "What?" Digger repeated the question, and his mother, ready to rant about her mad siblings, shifted and said, "Oh, that. You know, the grocers, the doctor's nurses, the people on TV. They're all so young. Why, the new pharmacist looks like a high school student. Everybody's getting younger. The whole world."

"Oh," said Digger, a little disappointed in the puzzle's simple answer. He saw what she meant. It was all about strangers, not family members, not friends. With that mystery solved, he and his mother traded goodbyes. They would see each other at Christmas.

Digger got up and looked down the corridor: all empty doors now. Bill seemed to have left. From the rooftop, a gull cried, and Digger imagined wind and elements, a disemboweled clam. At being alone, Digger felt a relief tinged with sadness.

Looking back into his office, he saw that Simba had raised her head to see what was up. Sharp ears shifting from frequencies near and far, Simba's wide-open dark eyes communicated that she was ready for whatever Digger had in mind.

"Let's go home, girl."

Chapter Thirteen: Audience Analysis

This advice cannot be overstated: you must consider your audience when writing a college essay. Of course, in general, your reader is just your teacher, maybe by extension the class, but not always. Especially the further you go in college, your audience will become more specific, more professional, but even in your freshman year, you need to think of your reader's needs and interests.

The fall semester's course schedule ended, finals got taken, last papers received grades, and the Christmas break beckoned and then began. Over the break, Digger had planned to finish a scholarly article about using music to help students remember grammatical problems, such as wordiness, run-ons, punctuation problems, anything related to editing. He knew the power of music, the way melodies could hover and haunt. When Anna left, she'd given one main reason, one main word: *free*. She'd said that she wanted to be free. Oh, how he had argued that she was! How, too, he had repeated that word "free" since then, every day, making up a little song that rhymed with the word: *Free to be, and free of me*. It had many verses, many playful melodies even, all sad, all initiated at even the most innocuous of times, for the word "free" showed up everywhere—often during news broadcasts, on advertisements (the land of the free, of course), in superficial conversations. After all, the son-of-a-bitching word fit almost any part of speech. With the passing years, Digger remembered less and less of Anna—the angles of her face, the tones of her voice—but the word "free" and its myriad melodies continually barked for his attention.

He learned to use music in his classes, and Digger had titled his article, his winter-break project, "Grammar Jam: Let the Music Play." So far, that was the extent of his piece, which required corroborating research (about music's effects). He had plenty of examples (grammar songs) and experience since he used Grammar Jam in class a couple of times per semester. To model the activity, he would sing the following lyrics to Simon and Garfunkel's "The Sound of Silence":

Semicolon you don't bend
To use you I must end
A statement and begin another
Perhaps with "therefore" or "however."
A soft period, you balance two main thoughts
Like a see-saw
Or sometimes items, in a complex list.

Students recognized the song, the melody, even decades after its release, so sometimes they would sing along when Digger transitioned into his stanza on colons, then commas, then dashes, and finally parentheses (and brackets). The song took a few minutes to sing. After sharing this model, Digger would let the students form groups and then build songs, some of which offered good advice and all of which brought laughter and collaboration. Digger understood his audience— college students: they wanted to learn (for the most part), but they did not want to sit passively and endure lectures.

For his article, Digger knew the audience, too, and they would expect more than just a lesson plan: scholarly readers wanted proof (research) that the activity was valid. After Christmas, Digger would find proof and plan his article. He had done it before, once a year or so, far more often than any of his peers, a fact that made Digger feel good about himself, that trickled nourishment to his ego, for he was a *writer*, not just a teacher, not a member of the those-who-can't-do-teach club. His peers rarely mentioned his continual flow of articles, though, and Digger no longer pointed them out as he once had—before Anna. He just seemed to care more back then, to want to share more, to create a sense of community. Now he communicated alone, having a pipeline to a scholarly source on higher education. Digger emailed the magazine's editor fairly often, and she rarely changed his words—a quality much admired in an editor, in his estimation.

With the arrival of Christmas, Digger's audience shifted to a seventy-three-year-old lady and a six- or seven-year-old dog, and while the latter appeared happy with everything Digger did or said, the former seemed far less in agreement. "Christmas is not like it used to be," declared Jean Diggerson, and then she elaborated on why: "Your father used to bring in a fresh spruce, a real tree." Digger had bought her a nice four-foot fake tree a few years earlier. "I can smell those pine needles like it was yesterday." He had bought her a pine-scented candle a couple years ago. "Your father would always buy me a nice piece of jewelry." He bought her opal earrings last Christmas. "And Emma! She would run about and sing carols. Even when she was a young lady, she would sing. We wouldn't have to listen to tapes." Digger had bought her a Christmas carols CD last year, too. "Now they're both gone and Christmas, too, Matthew. Christmas, too!"

Anna, too, Digger would add in his mind, allowing his mother's words to flow over him—like water off a duck's back, he continually reminded himself (black water)—and offering the conventional frown of agreement and commiseration. He missed his father and only sibling, too. Both had been taken by accidents way too soon, both in car crashes, separate ones no less. After his DWI or DUI, his mother wouldn't even speak to him—for about an hour. Then she bombarded him with "How Could You's" and reminders of his father's and sister's deaths. At least his mother still had two of her sisters, both close by, and an older brother, albeit one who could no longer hear at all. "What!" was pretty much all John Wilder ever said anymore. Later on, Digger would take his mother to the nursing home to see John; Carol and Mary would be there, too, sooner or later. In Acapulco-like layers, they would all tell Digger how pale he looked and how he needed to marry again. "I have Simba," he would retort, smiling, but the old women would just shake their heads, his mother joining in, too, so that Digger would think of three decrepit parrots bobbing on a branch. He would know that they were right, too, and that they all loved him.

They had loved Anna, too, and the head shaking back then had to do with the lack of niece, nephew, or grandchild. How often had he heard that he wasn't getting any younger? And since Anna's departure, why could none of these old people (his mother was the youngest sibling in the Wilder clan) remember Simba's name? They would pat the air above Simba's head and say, "Good dog, Good doggie." Guiltily, when visiting his family (after the three-hour drive to get there), Digger often wanted to get away, to be by himself, by himself with Simba.

Even his silent, empty cottage seemed welcoming after a few days with his family because it offered safety, peace, a pathway to the past, a timelessness atmosphere. The ocean's waves drew him inward, the gulls' manic sounds—laughter or screams?—rooted him to the earth, and Simba's calm presence and acceptance bathed him with gentle significance. Digger knew that the meaning of life—if one existed—was love, for he had experienced it: the soft, warm center, the jagged edges, and now the steady warm flow. Back from his Christmas visit to his mother's, Digger felt a page turning, his obsession with Tobias' killer fading, drifting off. He would make no more lists of suspects, conduct no more interviews with colleagues, visit the little detective no more. He would never find out how tall the policeman was (unless he ran into Doyle at the coffee shop). He would study music's effects on learning, take notes, note sources, and build his Grammar Jam article. He would tell his peers about this article, get them to sing his stanzas, connect with them more meaningfully. He would walk Simba on the beach each day, meditating in the karma of the waves and the pale winter sun. He would turn with the earth, not lower his head against it. He would treat the new year as a new beginning, not just as another morning.

Then he thought of Anna, of their love of this season, how they would decorate the tree and take winter walks on the beach. In his mind, the word "Anna" led down two paths, one warm and quiet, comforting, the other dark, deep, down to the black river flowing beneath Digger's consciousness. In that thick shadowed stew, Digger would drown himself, flow away, experience all the emotions that he normally kept in check: frustration, anger, confusion, righteousness, fear—and others. This dark path was silent, too, and as dangerous as wet leaves on a hillside. Up that slope, the path would come for Digger, opening without being seen, beckoning without being heard.

Thinking of the old years and of the new one coming, of another New Year's Eve alone, another without Anna, Digger went to the kitchen and grabbed a beer. Enjoying the cold metal feel and the expectation, he clicked down the tab but didn't drink, not yet, just looked out the back window at the little snow tornados beyond his green fence. The beach was almost empty, just swaths of thin whiteness here and there, the winds having swept most of the sand clean. The afternoon sky looked more like twilight, and Digger gazed unseeing at the heavens and took a swig of the Bud Light—cold and full and bracing. He heard Simba slump contentedly at his feet, but he kept his eyes on the layered sky. He drank again, wiped the sweet foam from his lips. For a long time, he stood at the window, looking both out and in, both at the present and the past. He had forgotten his new year's connection vows, lost touch with the future.

The Ocean View College campus was particularly deserted between Christmas and New Year's Eve. Most of the staff members had that time off, and so would have Dan Pinsky if not for a tumble and a two-week rehabilitation back in July. In August, he'd made up one week, and now, before the turn of the year, he trudged toward the Faculty Offices Building to fulfill that second week. The late afternoon sun blinded him but offered no warmth. The winds flung snow crystals about in tiny tornados that rose up to human height and burst. Dan the Man didn't mind these earthly obstacles, all created by God, but still he wanted to get this week over with. Since Professor Mann's death, work had been less enjoyable because nobody else really talked to him. Professor Diggerson would stop, but he didn't talk like Professor Mann used to. With him, Dan had hardly had to say a word, just listen to the wise life advice pouring out. It had been an education. As he fumbled with the front door keys, Dan Pinsky received a shock.

"Oh, you startled me," he said, turning to the hooded figure, who seemed to have appeared within one of those ice tornados. "Do you need to get into the building?"

Indeed, the other did. The other had to get into the building and retrieve some work. Just because the holidays had arrived, that didn't mean that the work stopped, did it? "Humanity must toil." That was what the other said, and Dan had to agree. Maybe this professor was more like Professor Mann than he had realized, thought the janitor, and he put his mind back on the keys: at least a dozen hung from a heavy ring, as though Dan were a dungeon master. Dan was proud of the keys, of the responsibility granted by access, so he held them up into the late-day sun and shook them not only to find the right key, but to announce his ownership of them all.

The hooded figure declined to admire the keys. Once inside, the two OVC employees took the elevator up, saying nothing much more than holiday greetings, and then the elevator dinged, stopping at the third floor. "I'll be working on the fourth floor for awhile," said Dan. "If you need my help, you know where to find me." The other smiled, waved, walked off down the Humanities corridor. The elevator doors closed, and Dan rose up.

On the third floor, the hooded figure backtracked and entered a conference room, cold and empty. Still hooded, Tobias Mann's killer stood motionless as if listening and then moved to the window, looked out at winter. While Digger's office window showed the campus' main quad, a big open area with intersecting pathways, the conference room's windows actually offered a better view: sweeping lawns, a little tree line, and then the ocean, that is, the bay's emptying out into the great Atlantic. Nothing moved out there; it was like a picture, an oil painting. Then the standing presence noticed a couple of soaring seagulls, far off, and one swooped by above, where the birds would perch like beach-bound buoys on the roof, casting out their muffled calls, a sound mixing anger, fear, and defiance, a sound void of love or compassion. The killer understood the sound, could feel its echoes and vibrations, but those feelings had to be controlled now. No mere gull, the other must become the Condor, with great wings, great power. *Pinsky—what does that fool know?* More than he realized, no doubt. *The idiot could be right above, right now,* up there cleaning an already clean floor, swooshing that mop he always carried back and forth, back and forth. Pinsky was a simple fool and easy to understand and to manipulate. Through the ceiling, the hooded figure summoned the janitor down and waited, just staring out the window, motionless.

But patience could last only so long. *Where is that dope?* The killer felt a sudden wave of frustrated anger, exited the conferences room, and stared down both halls, one then the other—nothing. With no one to gab at, the janitor was probably doing some actual work, *or more likely snoring with his big fat face on one of the reception couches, dreaming of his hero, the late great Tobias Mann. Not so great a man after all. None are! Not so smart or in control. None are! Professors, cops, doctors with their big words and waiting rooms, all meant to control the minions.* But control could be twisted, tightened. All it took was self-control and that link to the wild, where everything and everyone was connected, where minds could be penetrated, and that was really the key: understanding the person, knowing what he would do, having the strength and will to act, to fly like a great bird of prey. *Like the Condor.*

The hooded figure descended to the adjunct faculty office to wait (the door being open, of course, for what of consequence could an adjunct office possible hold?), and soon, from down the corridor, the elevator bell tinged. The figure retreated slowly through the office door, backwards, sinking into a chair like a big black spider. Before long, Pinsky's whistling dribbled down the hall, some tuneless thing, the gross noise growing gradually. *Probably some psalm, Pinsky's gathering at the river, no doubt.* Here he came now, standing in the doorway, just as planned.

"Still working, I see," said Dan the Man, his big body taking up nearly the entire doorway. "The Lord rewards those who work. Are you cold?"

The Condor laughed at that, a single, cold "Hah!" and turned to face the working man. "Yes, I am cold, but I have a joke for you."

"A joke," said Dan. "I like jokes."

"Do you want to hear it?" When Dan said that he did, the other rose smoothly up from the chair, as though the joke would require bodily gestures. The hooded killer took a step toward Dan Pinsky, a hopping flight.

"What are the three most dangerous wrestling holds?" The words "three" and "wrestling" were accented, given a hiss and a sizzle.

Dan lowered his head toward the mop handle, as though deep in thought. *Wrestling*, he thought, for that you must pin your opponent. "Holds?" he repeated to buy himself more time. From the hooded face, two pricks of light twinkled and flared out.

"The Half-Nelson," said the Condor, taking another half step, a little flight, just the twitch of a great wing, and Dan recognized the term "half-Nelson" although he couldn't remember why.

"The Full-Nelson," said the other, advancing, flying now, but the janitor didn't feel darkness coming, because he almost had the answer, because Dan the Man was focused on "Full Nelson," which he'd almost said right along with the joker.

"And the Father Nelson, you religious moron!" screamed the Condor, arcing a shining silver object into the janitor's big exposed chest, creating a drawn-out "Oooomph" and a little fountain of blood, a gentle red rain. The big man slumped backward, forcing the Condor to jerk upwards, to extract its deadly beak, which had done the job, oh, yes! Dan the Man lay dead on his own clean floor, still clutching the mop in his right hand.

Good, thought the other. *He'll have something to do in Hell.*

Chapter Fourteen: Repetition

Be very careful with repetition in college papers. Obviously, you should not repeat ideas or examples in a composition, because academic readers want to see new information as they read. However, college writers do need to repeat their body paragraph topics as they explain them in order to create unity in those paragraphs—a sense of oneness. Without unity, a paragraph's content could careen out of control, taking readers on a confusing ride. Thus, in terms of repetition, be wary and aware.

Dan Pinsky's body was found the night of his murder, for Campus Security had learned from its last encounter with death. This time, a patrolling officer noted the Faculty Offices Building's third-floor lights close to midnight, an incongruous image that reminded the young security man of the lit-up building from November, of nobody's checking on those lights and the macabre scene they had held. With January's winds blowing, *déjà vu* passed through Officer Timothy McDonald, a part-time rookie on the extremely small force, comprised of two full-time retired cops and four part-time want-to-be patrolmen, the ones who spent most of the time walking the campus.

After radioing back to the Security Shack, McDonald was told to "wait there" and "not to enter the building." That was fine with the young patrolman. Within two minutes, Officer Gloria Thomas arrived, bringing both guidance and apprehension, most clearly noted in her voice, described best as barked whispering.

"This doesn't look right. Why would one floor be lit up this late at night?"

"Maybe somebody forgot to turn it off," Officer McDonald whispered, too.

"Or maybe somebody turned it on. Maybe somebody's still up there. Did you try the door?"

"You told me not to go in."

"Well, we're going in now." But the door was locked this time. With the Mann incident, the door had been unlocked, giving the police a puzzle, which had never been solved. Either the killer had had a key and left the door unlocked, or the victim had mistakenly done so since a key to the outer door had been found in his pocket. Thinking of those possibilities, Officer Thomas worked through a big ring of her own keys, a mass of metal to draw the envy of Dan Pinsky, and fitted one into the front door, which swung open with a whispering swish. Both officers felt a change in the air, warmer to the body, colder to the mind. Officer McDonald's mouth hung open, his breath puffing out visibly in quick huffs. Officer Thomas breathed through her nose, looking slightly reptilian to her young colleague. Her nostrils flared and relaxed, expanded and deflated, reminding the rookie of some small creature's frightened heart, maybe a frog's. "Stay behind me," the woman declared, moving into the building. "We're going up."

Armed with only her wits and caution (OVC security officers were not allowed weapons), Officer Thomas led her subordinate up the stairs, turned on the landing, and up another flight, turn, flight, turn, flight—to the third floor. Through the landing's square window, both officers could see that both corridors were illuminated. They hesitated, both minds focused on the original scene of the crime, the left corridor, and then Thomas peeked through the window— nothing but furniture.

"Slowly," she commanded, but McDonald hardly heard her, didn't need to, for all that drew him on was his leader's slow movements forward, a connecting line made of one part courage, two parts cowardice, and a generous helping of ignorance. The two passed into the open area where a pair of empty secretaries' desks squatted—one for History, the other Humanities—and Thomas glanced behind both, under both.

"Touch nothing," stated the ex-cop, not looking at the youth. "Stay behind me." Bent as though leading with a handgun (which the experienced cop had never longed for more), Officer Thomas looked first down the Humanities corridor because that was where trouble arrived last time, and she noticed a shape on the floor three-quarters of the way down. Even at this distance, she knew what she was seeing, a body, probably a dead body, but still she called out to the motionless form. "Police! Identify yourself! Police!" In the empty hallways, the words just bounced about and died. The shape down the hallway failed to do as told.

"Listen," whispered Thomas again. "We're backing out of here, right now, right down those same stairs, and we're touching nothing. We need to call the OVP."

That was good news for Officer McDonald, who'd just now been re-evaluating his future in law enforcement. His eyes looked like two white poker chips with little black centers, and Officer Thomas thought irrationally of a goat. When the two reached the outside world, the woman immediately used her radio; she knew the number, having worked for the Ocean View Police force until her retirement three years past. Lacking his elder colleague's experience, Officer McDonald just breathed and breathed, discharging his emotions in streams of white carbon dioxide that faded like cheap colorless fireworks into the dark.

The effects of murder repeated—in the same building, down the same corridor, at the same spot, basically—were dramatic. The story went national, as serial killers' exploits often did (when the "right" people were murdered, thought Digger, watching events unfold on TV), with headlines like "Killer College" and "Ocean View Murder." Reporters flocked the campus, but because the second killing took place during winter break, they found few people to interview (no students, thus losing the youth angle) and gradually disappeared. At first, OVC's administrators were frazzled, lamenting all the bad publicity and fearing the worst: mass student withdrawal. However, while some students did not return for the spring semester, attendance actually rose, especially in the criminal justice fields, and when Digger heard about this fact, he imagined bright-eyed recruits with dreams of solving the murders and single-handedly catching the FOB Murderer, as the culprit was soon labeled by students via emails.

The Faculty Offices Building was off limits during most of January, an inconvenience for few since spring classes did not begin until the end of that month. With the help of police, OVC's administrators had a video camera installed (hidden) down the Humanities hallway, and all buildings on campus (including dorms) now had technology that took pictures of people when they entered the front doors. The school's president took to the airwaves to laud this expensive security addition because Ocean View College would apparently go to "unprecedented lengths to ensure the safety of the students— and the staff."

On the staff, the janitor's murder had a numbing effect. Jessica Williams decided to take early retirement (even though she was only thirty-nine, just under Digger's own age). Don Domberg, now voted in as Chairperson, set up a winter meeting (in the school's library) to cover all the known information about the killings (not much) and to allay teachers' fears (not as strong as expected, probably since Pinsky's murder took place during vacation, along with the fact that the janitor wasn't well known or, to be honest, well liked). Many staff members never saw the maintenance crew, which worked after four in the afternoon, but that schedule shifted after the second murder. Now, janitors worked nine to five because nobody wanted to be left alone in OVC buildings after the sun went down. With images of litigation rioting in their heads, administrators concurred. More meetings arose, like fat spring mushrooms (stale and full of air), but not much more was administratively decided—other than the need for a steady hand through these turbulent waters. Each administrator imagined being the captain of that hand.

As for Digger himself, Pinsky's death reignited his obsession with Tobias' murder, for obviously the same killer had returned. Obviously, too, certain suspects didn't fit the janitor's murder. How could George North, a student, have gotten into the building during winter intersession? For that matter, how could Amy Mann have done so? She was always an unlikely suspect, anyway, but Digger still could not release her name from suspicion. She could have had an accomplice, her son, her gardener. Amy and the hit man! Maybe Pinsky knew something, having been a confidant of her husband. Along with his mop and never-ending dialogue, maybe Pinsky carried a secret.

Digger acknowledged that deep down he wanted the wife to be the killer, but he also focused now on two remaining suspects, both colleagues: Bill Jacobs and Paul Smith. After his enjoyable brainstorming session with Bill, he had dropped him as the killer, but now Digger reassessed the facts and decided that Bill could be wearing a mask. Anyone could. Look at his own masks titled 'Peace' and 'Contentment.' Digger wondered if the little detective, Doyle, had come to the same conclusions and underlined, "Matthew Diggerson" on the computerized list—if it weren't already accented.

By telephone, reporters harassed Digger and many other Humanities professors. Tiring of humanity's superficial shadows and relentless verbiage, Digger decided not to attend Pinsky's funeral, but read online that it was well graced, mainly by murder junkies who didn't even know Dan the Man. A week later, reporters announced new and startling information that answered one of Digger's old coffee-shop questions: the killer had needed just one knife blow to kill each man. Thereafter, the news gnats dubbed him (or her, but increasingly the likelihood was male) the Single-Stroke Killer, a moniker requiring daily updates even when not warranted. Apparently, Detective Doyle and his superiors considered the one-strike evidence to be necessary for public safety, that to withhold it would be negligent. Lawsuits, thought Digger. Everything was done to prevent being held accountable and sued. Clearly, the pleasant community of Ocean View housed a dangerous, capable madman.

Digger had troubled dreams. At least once per week, he awoke in a sweat, having witnessed a repeated image: Anna, her arms outstretched to him and his to her. *Anna, Anna, Anna*, he called out, but she would drift away, fade away, and he would awaken to the terrible emptiness—except for Simba, usually laid out at the base of his bed, slumbering peacefully or half alert with one ear raised and both eyes at half mast. These dreams made Digger question his own sanity. How could a person still be so wrecked after seven and a half years? In many ways, Anna had left him just last week, for that was how it felt: as though she had walked away recently. Then he remembered how it really was back then, the numb disbelief, the way he waited for her to return at night even though she'd told him she was leaving, that she wanted a divorce, *freedom*, that her life wasn't what she expected, that she wanted more—but not him.

The FOB killings sparked more Anna dreams, too, and for several nights after Dan Pinsky's demise, Digger awakened to darkness, to despair. But Anna wasn't taken by a killer; she was the killer, a realization that did nothing to lighten his mood. The killer, he thought, must feel a similar darkness, the same sense of loss and despair, but why? He thought of Paul Smith and the way he seemed to have changed, or had he? Bill was the same, but that was not necessarily a note in his favor. Don Domberg entered his mind, too, but now Don had control. Why would he need to kill a janitor? *The secret?* Omar Johns' round head floated past Digger's mind—his thin neck and cunning smile. Then the Stranger surfaced in

Digger's thoughts. Was he really a stranger or a known stranger, an oxymoron? His mother's philosophy, now simplified, drifted past: a young wave of strangers. Was the killer a young stranger? Digger thought of the two newest and youngest full-timers—Todd and Jolie—and then of the younger part-timers, even of Elena, who looked young but must have been close to thirty-five, even past it. How could she kill a giant janitor?

These questions, images, and anxieties played out each night as January crawled by, one day bright and cold, the next cloudy with flurries. Digger finished his scholarly article and emailed it off, planned his spring courses, took beach walks with Simba. For his resolution to connect more often and more deeply, he made no progress. In winter's depths, the gulls dipped and screamed and bobbed and waited.

Chapter Fifteen: Run-Ons

Also known as comma splices and fused sentences, a run-on is just two unconnected statements—a common but destructive error. When the reader gets part way into the second thought, he or she recognizes it (the second statement) and realizes the lack of a connection. Thus, the error interrupts the flow of communication and causes the reader to return to the second thought's beginning. To avoid that distraction, just read your sentences aloud, listening for unlinked statements—i.e., spots that might need an "and" or "but," perhaps a period or semicolon, that oft misused mark.

At January's end, the Spring Semester began with an atmosphere that Digger and his composition colleagues described as "creepy." For one thing, clouds obstructed the sky and pushed down on each individual, creating claustrophobia as the heavenly masses thickly rolled about, occasionally showing dark underbellies that threatened snowfall but failed to deliver it. The clouds squatted so low that the tops of OVC's four-story brick buildings seemed smudged, and gulls disappeared into the swirling gloom— swallowed up, their cries muffled. Students and faculty walked about with heads down, the teachers bunched up against the winds, the students mainly glued to their cell phones. When people met each other and tried to trade thoughts, the statements came out disjointed, one leading to another without transitions. Since no one knew quite what to say or how to avoid the subject of murder, teachers and staff and students blabbed on about the cold weather, the lack of snow, the busy schedules, the students who didn't work hard enough, the professors who assigned too much work— whatever popped knifeless into their minds. Finally, they accepted the unconnected thoughts about the killer, the killings, and then the theories came out.

The students broached the subject before the teachers did, and Digger had expected this interest. In fact, over the winter break, he had searched the Web for articles about serial killers, wanting to find two different approaches for his first main paper, a simple (but still challenging) summary assignment. After clicking on several links, he had decided on two fairly short articles, one offering statistics and logic, the other relying on appeals to fear and inflammatory language (some clear logical fallacies). The former writer argued that a person had almost no chance of being a serial killer's victim, the second author suggested that shadows lurked behind every door, that meeting a madman was not a matter of "if" but "when." Because this second article exaggerated and offered little evidence, Digger hoped that these readings would lessen students' fears about being on a campus where two murders had taken place in approximately two months.

During that first week of the semester, Digger said hello to Omar Johns, to his flashing teeth, twice, both times within the Faculty Offices Building, where in the previous dozen years he hadn't seen any administrator even once. Johns had apparently taken it upon himself to guard the crime scene and prevent any more bad OVC press. Digger considered telling the administrator that all press was good press, and then about warning the thin man not to lurk in the FOB after dark, but he offered neither point because the thoughts both seemed flippant.

With the transition to February, Digger read his students' summary papers and was pleased: the students (nearly all) not only understood both arguments, but also recognized the flaws in the second article. Some explained those unsupported manipulations in their essays' body paragraphs, getting off purpose (i.e., summarizing the articles' main and supporting points), but Digger treated these transgressions as a teaching opportunity. For his second assignment, a more analytical analysis of a writer's language use, Digger found two more "killer" writings, one a short story, the other a song, giving students a choice in topics. Most chose the song, probably because it was shorter, and again, in general, Digger liked the resulting compositions, which took his classes into March. The occasional spring-like days dispelled some of the shadows that had lain across the campus.

Nevertheless, every day Simba accompanied Digger to work, waiting for him in his office or curled up behind the new secretary's desk (Gloria Swanson had transferred over from the Psychology Department). Gloria showed no fear (not even in early February, closer to the janitor's death), walked the hallways often, stopped and socialized when doors were open. A big woman, Gloria made her presence felt, but in a nice way overall. Digger noted that she talked in run-ons, one statement leading to another with no connections and almost no pauses, like a female Dan the Man without the Lordly references. Maybe she was in fact afraid, thought Digger, and she used words to control or conceal feelings—a pretty common tactic. Digger liked Gloria and even her string of statements, which along with Simba returned life to the building. Although missing Jess Williams as a friend, a work comrade, Digger did not miss the haunted look stapled on her face. And maybe she was the killer, as Bill had joked; maybe the killer had run away.

Indeed, nothing shocking happened as the semester rolled into March and reached the half-way point, Spring Break, although one incident did bother Digger: looking out the FOB's conference room one late afternoon, he had seen a person down by the water. Too far for identification, the solitary stroller had reminded Digger of George North, the hair and gait, and his mind kept returning to that possibility. Finally, one day during his office hours, he dialed the four-digit number to the Administration Building.

"Registrar," came a familiar female voice, Joan Leonard's.

"Joan, this is Matt Diggerson. How's things going?"

"Always crazy here, Matt."

"Do you have time to check on a student for me?"

"Always for you." Joan Leonard always said these three words, probably dozens of times each day.

"His name's George North. He was in my 102 class last semester. I just wondered if he transferred. Just curious."

Silence drifted along the line, but Digger thought he could hear key strokes. "George North," Joan announced, adding "not a hard name to spell." Then she said, "Still here, Matt. Would you like to contact him?"

No he wouldn't, but Digger responded instead, "No thanks, Joan. I was just curious." He thanked her again and hung up, thought about George a bit more. Determined the unlikelihood of a student's getting into the Faculty Office Building after hours not only once, but twice. Then he thought of the Big Two, as two of the adjuncts had become. Since both Bill and Paul taught on morning schedules, Digger had seen neither man all semester, but they rose up in his imagination often.

On the last Friday afternoon before Spring Break, Digger discovered one of them in the adjunct office as the sun started to dip in the still cloudy sky.

"Paul," he said, stopping in the door to the shared office, empty now except for Paul Smith. "What are you doing here? I haven't seen you all semester."

"Wrapping up some work," the older man stated, and Digger noticed dark pouches under his eyes. Paul seemed to be aging; maybe he was sick. "My wife's tired of me, too," added Paul Smith. "She told me to go away." He laughed at that, one harsh sound, more like a cough than mirth.

"So did mine," said Digger, thinking that a little self-abuse might buoy his skeletal peer, and after admitting it, Digger actually felt okay—an inch or two of growth after only seven and a half years.

But the other man failed to respond to Digger's grim joke, at least not outwardly. "Where's your shadow?" he asked instead, continuing to shuffle through papers on his desk. On cue, Simba strolled into the adjunct office from Digger's and walked right up to Paul, sniffing his pant leg, her tail wagging slowly. Paul patted Simba's head.

"Don't mind her," said Digger. "Simba only bites Republicans."

Again, no laugh or smile, no recognition of Digger's words. "I need one of these," Paul decreed, almost to himself more than to Digger. Because Paul Smith appeared vacant, body and mind in different places, Digger wanted his hands off of Simba.

Digger said that dogs came highly recommended, and hearing his voice, Simba looked over her shoulder at him, her big mouth breaking open into a grin. "Woof," she said, her sound muffled as always, sort of a grunt, appealing. Digger tried to catch her eye with a quick head nod toward the door.

Staring down at the hound, Paul Smith said, "You can count on these, can't you? Dogs."

"You can. Simba's basically always happy, always good company. She's a good friend." Digger's thoughts trailed off, then his words. He was not sure what the other man would say next, where his mind would go. Paul seemed lost in thought, petting Simba with one hand, holding papers in the other. Digger nodded again to catch Simba's eye, but the dog appeared content at present, sort of sleepy.

"How are your students doing this semester?" asked Digger, adding "Can you believe we're halfway through already?"

"And nobody's been murdered," replied Paul, barking again, once, and finally looking up, making Digger think of a zombie. Simba stopped wagging. Not finding any words, Digger motioned Simba to come, using another head nod. Awake and aware, forever checking her human for clues, Simba lumbered up and ambled to the door. Digger detected a slight odor, thought at first that Simba must have rolled in something, but then realized that it came from the other man. Digger rationalized that the days were warming up, and he contemplated pointing out the problem, a hard one to broach, a fellow human's lack of personal hygiene. With no words forming, though, Digger and his dog stood in the doorway, Digger facing Paul, thinking of that horrible little smell, Simba staring into the empty, darkening hallway, not interested in any human stench now. Paul had gone back to his papers.

"Any plans for spring break?" Digger expected a quick "no."

"Oh, I have plans. Plenty to do still. I have plans, and I'll let you know."

Digger recognized a threat, but how could that be? Did Paul's plans have anything to do with him? What plans?

"What plans?"

"I'll let you know," Paul said, and he looked straight at Digger in the doorway. The older man's eyes looked like holes. Then Smith's mouth ripped open in sunken glee, apparently, and Digger noted with shock that one of his colleague's teeth had fallen out. Behind his top left canine, a blank space. It made that canine tooth look bigger, sharper. The black cube space caused the leering grin to look unbalanced, even wild. A smile that would unleash howling laughter, cascades of it. But Smith's mouth was silent.

Digger decided to let Paul's plans go and get out. "Well, I guess we'll be going, Paul. Have a great break. Say hello to your wife." He'd forgotten her name, Debbie maybe, forgotten even if Paul Smith had children. Smith's mouth closed up, like a big clam, but he continued to watch Digger in the doorway. Simba watched the strange, staring man; she seemed ready to voice her opinion about him.

"I told Pinsky a joke once," the seated man then said out of nowhere, a thought connected only in his mind, a statement that nevertheless jarred Digger, the reference to a murdered man making him mute. "He didn't get it, of course. The big dope." Then nothing more—silence.

Chapter Sixteen: Taking a Stance

In a way, every college paper is an argument since you're implying that readers should believe what you say, but most academic assignments involve simple explanations, not arguments. In composition courses, though, many instructors assign position papers, requiring students to take a stance about some issue, to confront opposing points to that claim, and to provide valid evidence in support of it. While these papers do not represent assignments from other fields, they do show students the importance of extended analysis, both of a topic and of the audience.

Spring Break was uneventful, except that the local paper printed an article about Digger and Simba, titled "Keep Your Dog Close." It offered a nice picture of a grinning Simba, but Digger thought that he himself looked silly, sort of guilty even, as he squatted by his dog in the photo. The photographer had told Digger to smile, and although he thought that he had, the picture showed no teeth, just a little oval in Digger's mouth, as though he'd just been punched in the gut or caught in the act of something, maybe drinking and driving. He kept a copy of the article but cut out the picture because it reminded him of Paul Smith's hideous grin. That led to thoughts of Detective Doyle and to whether he'd seen the piece. The writer had offered an upbeat article about the positive effects that Simba had on the "still reeling" OVC community (functioning beneath the threat of the Single-Stroke Killer) and went a little over the top, thought Digger, wondering if the story seemed too good to be true, so good as to hide the killer, the dog-owner himself! After that piece, all the hard news breaking up into soft fluff, reporters had no longer stalked the campus since the murders appeared to have drifted into history—at least for the outside world. The scribes would return on anniversaries for quotations, of course, to keep the memories flowing.

Digger knew, however, that his students were still fascinated by the deaths, by their close proximity to the national events, and none seemed worried for their own safety. Like suburban residents watching urban carnage on the news, the students appeared to consider the killings to be someone else's problem—teachers, old people—not their own. To harness their enthusiasm after Spring Break, Digger assigned a position paper about the killings—in short, a 'Who Done It?' essay. He warned against the use of anyone's name, offering instead general categories:

- A colleague
- A staff member
- A student
- A family member
- A stranger
- (someone else)

Each writer had to choose one category and argue logically for it, confronting opposing views (people who would choose another category) and providing evidence (mainly hypothetical, but also quotes from the first two papers' projects). If George North had still been one of Digger's students, he would not have created this assignment, worried about flippant sarcasm, but North had moved on to other courses, other paths. In fact, other than that long-distance possible sighting, Digger had not come across George even once this semester, didn't know if he'd decided to leave OVC or not—probably not. Probably he would graduate with a business degree, make buckets more money than a composition teacher, marry someone like Amy Mann, and have three kids who despised everything about him—except his money. And so the cycle would begin again. None of

Digger's current students resembled George, mocking and mysterious, and for that the professor was grateful.

During the first class (his pre-noon 101 course) after Spring Break, mid March, Digger introduced the assignment, created groups of three, and assigned a pros/cons exercise to generate ideas. In other words, each trio—assigned to a single category of suspects—had to generate points for and points against that category, doing so in just ten minutes. Within five, most trios seemed to be done, so to keep the cell phones from emerging, Digger called for presentations and jotted the ideas on the board. Since "a stranger" offered the most "pros," Digger wrote this topic sentence on the board: "For two main reasons, a stranger is the killer."

"This topic sentence would lead to a cause-effect body paragraph," he explained, "and that's an effective plan when you're arguing." Then he covered what he wanted each trio to do—i.e., to add to the TS, sentence by sentence, in order to build its paragraph—and what the students would win: three free minutes for the "best" (most clear and specific, as usual) in each added sentence category. To start, he called for the first structural point for the "stranger" topic sentence, but he offered no more information than that, because he wanted to see how much Spring Break had affected their learning. The trios all seemed productively busy, talking, jotting down words, and before long, the six groups sent emissaries to the board:

1. The victims were not related, so that shows the killer did not know them.
2. First, the murders have stopped, this implies that the stranger has moved on.
3. A colleague or student would not be capable of killing.
4. Although the killings both took place in the same building, the two people were different: a professor and a janitor.

5.   Firstly, the killings were crimes of opportunity, which a stranger could have committed.

6.   A stranger could have used a boat to get on campus.

Looking at these statements, Digger was glad to see specific reasons, but organizational points had to be clear, too.

"These are all good ideas," he announced, "but only two provide clarity because only two offer transitional phrasing. Remember that ST's, structural points, begin shifts, so you must help the reader to see that shift. Here, we're going from the topic sentence to its first ST, so which two clearly show that shift?"

Two of the trios—groups two and five—enthusiastically referred to themselves, and the other students grudgingly agreed. Dividing the three minutes between the two winning trios, Digger next called for an illustration, giving the groups a choice to follow either the second or fifth structural point. He left those two on the board (in the second example, he replaced the comma with a semicolon) and erased the four others. As the class progressed—some examples showing nice specific content, others providing just broad information—Digger requested an explanation next and then the second structural point. This time, all six of the trios provided transitions—"In addition" (twice), "Secondly," "Second," "Next," and "Another reason"—and all the second reasons would work. Digger experienced the glow of successful teaching.

The active lesson continued, and before trios started to leave, having earned free minutes for clear and specific efforts, most of the cause-effect body paragraph (two showing different first-reason sections) appeared, sentence by sentence. Before any group exited, though, Digger said that students could use the ideas from the board, but not the exact sentences.

He repeated the exercise in two of his other 101 classes, and in both, the Stranger was the anointed killer, a fact that surprised Digger, made him think. Perhaps he was not being fair to suspect Paul or Bill. Then he remembered how "strange" Paul had been (and looked) lately—and that Bill had always been odd. Sitting in his office later that day, absentmindedly stroking Simba, Digger decided to contact the little detective once more, and what was more, he vowed to stop drinking. He would have no beer until the killer was found, maybe not even after that. The headaches, the fuzzy memories, the weakness: from *this* point forward, they were ended. He would help Doyle. However, before he could pick up the phone to solidify and symbolize this new stance, Gloria Swanson appeared in the doorway. Due to her suddenness, Simba said "woof," and the new Humanities secretary laughed openly. "I like you, too," she said to the dog, and Digger liked that. He liked people who talked directly to dogs.

"Digger," she now said to him. "We've known each other for a long time." That seemed like a stretch to him, but he had always said hello when passing through the Psych building. "I've watched you retreat into this dog." Digger's eyebrows rose. "A very nice dog, but a dog. Now, Elena ..." Digger groaned inside. "You know that she's been dating Professor Watkins, right?" Digger, remembering the funeral wave, nodded that he did even though he didn't. "He's not for her, Digger. I worked in Psych for many years, and let me tell you that those professors are all in fact a little crazy. I loved them all, but a mother loves all her kids, too, right? Even the wackos and goofballs. That Bill Watkins has a pretty big head, and your head's been too little too long." Digger thought of Omar Johns' round head and smiled. "Now don't you laugh at me, Professor Diggerson. I'm only looking out for you, and for Elena. You two would make a cute couple."

Then Gloria stopped and just stared at Digger, who held his palms up suggesting helplessness, and then at Simba, who wagged her tail. "Okay, Professor Diggerson, lecture's over," she said, adding, "Bye, Simba." Frowning at Digger again, she vanished from the doorway.

Digger sat and watched a sunbeam full of swirling dust, thought of other worlds, tiny golden ones. After Gloria's good-natured lecture and abrupt departure, the office felt especially closed in, almost prison like. *Well, then, another door closed.* The possibility of time shared with Elena was snuffed out. Who could blame her? Empty lives needed filling. For almost a decade, Digger had thought of his own life as an illustration of loss. His father's sudden end had brought shock and the realization of time as a creeping, hidden menace. His sister's death carried the same shock but sadness, too, a feeling of blank chapters. But nothing had ripped at his innards like Anna's freedom speech, like the first time he'd returned home to a cold harbor void of her body and soul and earthly possessions—all swept clean. Nothing symbolized loss like that. Digger sometimes thought of existence after that crushing, empty moment as a long cry, a howl to the night and stars, a laser of pain that would shoot across America and cause a little dog's ears in Manhattan to twitch, a row of Nebraska corn to ripple and shiver, a child's eyes in Colorado to snap open from a dream, covers to be pulled up to chin, a straight shot of sorrow that would pierce the heavens and scream toward the universe's mad expansion, chasing the end of all things. Several years since the Anna-cry's inception, Digger could no longer hear the attenuated despair, but he could always feel it. His black river, like a lake of oil beneath the earth's crust, that was where Digger had tried to drown the sound of the pain, but it would not stay dead.

His office and the Humanities corridor were as silent and still as a tomb. Even Simba slept like the dead with none of her common dream twitches or human-like snoring. Still, her warmth pulled Digger back to the present. A little annoyed by Gloria's intervention, a little touched by her efforts, Digger reached down and stroked Simba's ears (she stretched her short arms and legs, one pair forward, one pair back, and contracted back into repose) and thought about Elena, about the big-headed Will Watkins, but soon Paul and Bill slipped back in, then Doyle. *Doyle*. Maybe Digger could get the little detective to stand up, and Officer Tanner drifted through his mind, too.

Chapter Seventeen: Parallelism

This concept (the same part of speech used side by side) becomes especially important with professional writing, which often requires visuals, such as lists and tables, since ideas stand out more clearly when set up in parallel form—e.g., noun beginnings, commands, "ing" starts, etc. In college papers, parallel phrasing can help you to add rhythm, power, and variety to some of your sentences, but do not overuse it, because too much will appear as an exaggerated style, actually damaging your credibility, making you look self-absorbed to the reader.

Before going to see Doyle, Digger took Simba home, fed her, and said, "I'll be back soon." March had brought longer days, yet the sun could not penetrate this Monday's heavy blanket of grey clouds, stuck motionless to the sky, lumpy, like old oatmeal. As usual, on the way to his pickup, Digger glanced at the ocean, today seeing nary a whitecap in the sleeping sea. Digger liked waves, so he turned away faster than usual, turned to face his concerns and responsibilities.

At the station, Officer Jowles was back.

"Where's Officer Tanner?" asked Digger, and the burly cop replied, "I hear that question a lot." Instead of answering it, Jowles motioned Digger toward Doyle's corridor with a quick head nod, apparently one of the unhealthy-looking cop's mannerisms.

Doyle greeted Digger with a half-smile and a full two-pump handshake, but he didn't get up. Apparently, the little detective did most of his detecting from this chair and desk. Digger apologized for taking up more of the policeman's time with his "amateur-hour hypotheses."

"You must tell your students that when they're building their papers no ideas are bad, that all could help them to build that paper, and that's how any investigation operates. We appreciate your interest and your hypotheses."

That was a long response for Doyle, so Digger felt like less of a nuisance, more like a fellow sleuth. He warmed up to the short cop.

"I've been thinking," said Digger, "and my students have, too. I've given them an assignment, a 'Who-Done-It?' paper, and most of them think that a stranger is the killer." He paused, expected the detective to judge that assignment, maybe to say something about appropriateness, but Doyle just nodded once for him to go on. "I have a list of their reasons." Digger had the list ready, so he handed it over:

1. Killings have stopped.
2. Faculty and students not capable of murder.
3. Victims too different—one professor, one janitor.
4. Easy access to campus—by boat to avoid security.
4. Not a family member (the usual suspect in murder).
5. Easy access to Faculty building (before the new locks).
6. Weapon suggests transient, not a gun owner.
7. Nothing stolen, suggesting madman, not educated person.
8. Single-Stroke Killer must be large, would stand out on campus.

As Doyle read, Digger continued, "The newspapers told about the knife, of course. I've had them research the killings. I haven't told them any of my own concerns or any of *our* dialogue—yours and mine. They don't know that I've been to see you twice. I think I'm as obsessed with murder as they are." Digger stopped; Doyle kept reading.

"Some of these ideas are pretty logical," said Doyle at last. "Family members *are* the usual suspects. Society fears the stranger, yet he typically only takes your money, not your life. Loved ones do that, and your students' 'easy access' points are valid, too. The campus is pretty vulnerable. And it's true that nothing was stolen. You have some good thinkers here."

"I have acted on behalf of the devil's advocate," replied Digger, regretting at once that description, thinking that it should have been relabeled the angel's advocate. "In other words, I've questioned their logic, especially the point about who's capable of murder."

"You think that a professor or student is capable?" asked Doyle.

"Not a student, not any longer, although I suppose that psychosis begins at conception, basically, and that it can manifest itself at any age. I suppose some of my past students have had psychological problems, that they've hidden them. I've had thousands of students. We all hide problems, don't we?"

"You seem to be thinking of one particular person," responded Doyle, and Digger realized, once again, that although the two men seemed to be working side by side, parallel, the little detective was actually steering the conversation, that Digger was in the hands of a professional, a shrewd interviewer.

Digger began his speech: "My office, the corridor, still has a feeling about it, but I suppose that's common and will never really change. But it still feels threatening, despite the camera at the front door. I've taken to smiling as I enter that building—silly. But the Humanities corridor is not a place to smile. I trust all of my peers—except one—and I want to tell you why because I'm not sure the murders have ended."

"Who do you suspect?" Doyle looked at his computer screen, and Digger realized that *he* was in there, in a file, probably called "Diggerson OVC" or something like that. Doyle asked if the suspect was Bill Jacobs.

"No," stated Digger. "Not really," he amended. "Bill is a bit odd, angry sometimes, no friend to either Tobias or Dan Pinsky, but I've talked to him about the killings, and he seems honest to me. In fact, his main flaw is honesty. I don't suspect him anymore."

"Then you've narrowed to Paul Smith," concluded Doyle after consulting his computer screen, and Digger nodded that he had.

"Yes," he said, continuing before Doyle could ask him why. "Before Dan's death, I had a long talk with him outside my office, and Dan went on and on about Tobias and who wanted to kill him. It was a fairly long list." Digger paused, expecting the detective to compare Pinsky's list to Digger's, but Doyle said nothing, just waited.

"Anyway," added Digger, "Paul was there that day, in his office, with his door closed. He must have heard Pinsky's accusations against him, against a lot of the teachers, and I think he—Paul—was the only one there that day. It was late in the afternoon, and I had just talked with Paul before he closed his door. Anyway, Dan showed up, and Dan is loud, was loud. I know that Paul was in the adjunct faculty office and that he must have heard every word. That could be a motive, and why did both killings occur down that corridor? My students had an answer for that. They said that Pinsky knew something about Tobias'—Professor Mann's—murder, so he was targeted in the Faculty Offices Building. They argued that the corridor was just a coincidence, that the janitor could have been killed anywhere in that building, that the killer—a stranger, they think—was comfortable with the Humanities corridor because he had struck there before. He had killed there successfully before, so why not do so again?"

Doyle nodded his head once, pursed his lips (thin to thinner), kept quiet.

"Something's wrong with Paul Smith," continued Digger. "I've known him for a decade, and he's depressed now, seems worn down. He's not the same, and he thought that Tobias was going to fire him. That's a bit of an assumption, but maybe he snapped. I would think that almost every murder takes that, the snap. It happened before, too, something to do with a student. I've never found out exactly what. Did you find out?"

Doyle looked thoughtful, his eyes not focused on anything in the room. "I'm going to tell you something, Professor Diggerson, but I don't want you to repeat it. This information has not been given to the press. You and I are operating along parallel lines. We found blood in Paul Smith's office, the one for part-time faculty. Just a little, a thin spray, but it tells us that the killer stood in the doorway of that office when he, or she, stabbed Mr. Pinsky. It was the janitor's blood, not the killer's. This fact could support your concerns over Professor Smith, and I suppose that I'm telling you now so that you can keep your guard up. Again, tell no one this information about the blood. I'm telling you for your own safety. The blood does not provide proof; it offers evidence against no one person, would not be effective in court. However, we are beginning to focus our investigation along the lines you have suggested. Keep your eyes and ears open when you're in your office."

"Of course, that evidence could be a coincidence, too," said Digger, processing the new facts, as much to himself as to the little detective. "Dan could have been cleaning that office. Anyone could have snuck up on him."

"Policemen do not trust coincidences."

"Nor do teachers," said Digger, and then he said it again, quieter: "Nor do teachers." Then he felt a little foolish for the repetition and said nothing.

Detective Doyle picked up the thread. "We are keeping an eye on that corridor, Professor Diggerson, but you need to be vigilant, too, and contact me whenever you have information. Even the littlest piece can break a case, and we need that piece."

Digger recognized the dismissal again, so he stood up and reached out his hand. "Thank you," he said, meaning it, and Detective Doyle took his hand, shook it twice again (must be a new mannerism, from one pump to two), and remained seated.

"Just one more thing," said Digger. "Amy Mann—why did she never call the police the night of Tobias' death? Can you tell me that? I've wondered about it."

The little detective half smiled, and Digger thought, *this man understands obsession.* "She thought that her husband was asleep in the guest bedroom. She thought that he was angry with her, and she said that she'd gone to bed early and gotten up late. We looked into her son quite carefully, too. He's going to inherit quite a bit of money, but we never suspected the wife, not really."

Digger thanked the other man and left the station, realizing for certain that Amy Mann was not the murderer, that Tobias' wife never killed him. He could let that obsessive desire go now, for the little detective had confided in him, had taken his name from the list. Digger felt close to the truth.

Chapter Eighteen: Conclusions

Exit fairly quickly, but leave your readers thinking: that's how you want to conclude your college essays. Ironically, while some students use questions to begin their papers, that rhetorical tactic actually works much better to end an essay because there it forces readers to answer the interrogative, keeping the student's paper in their minds. These questions must be interesting, though, not simple "Yes" or "No" ones. They should extend the thesis, going beyond the essay's purpose to issues and angles important to readers' lives.

Digger's black pickup was not in the dirt driveway beside the cottage, so where could the bastard be? *Out hunting me! No, that's not how it works.* The stooped man switched off his car, but the engine bubbled on and clonked a few times, refusing to die. *Stop it*, Paul Smith screamed, but maybe those words formed just in his own head, he decided, and he sat still in the old car until his breathing settled. *Time for a trade in.* Perhaps he would upgrade to a certain small pickup truck, and that thought made Smith happy, led him to think of Debra in the passenger seat and between them a nice dog, that nice little hound with the name of a lion. *Simba.* Debra would want Simba, she would not complain. Paul Smith looked at Digger's cottage, at the two windows that flanked the front door, but no dog's head appeared in either one. *Maybe the dog's out with Digger.*

Stepping out of the old station wagon and straightening up, feeling the same old creaks and pains, Smith listened for a dog's barking but heard just background wind, a sort of humming. *Not much of a watchdog you have there, Digger.* As he stepped toward the green front door, the gaunt man used both hands to raise his grey sweatshirt's hood over his head.

The edges of the hood narrowed his vision and his focus, and after a few steps, the man stood before the door, but didn't knock. *Who's going to answer? The dog?* A gull cried, and the visitor followed its lonely, drifting call around the house down a welcoming path of paving stones. *Digger did a nice job with these.* The hooded man gave the pretty backyard a sweeping and appraising look. The frozen cardinals announced a balmy 50 degrees. *Nice.* Digger's backyard was flanked by fencing and shrubbery, secluded from prying eyes. He was alone.

Smith's heart pounded when he noticed the dark eyes looking up at him through the bottom pane of glass in the back door. "Oh, ho! There's the lion dog! Hello, Simba! I've come to see your master. I've come at last, thank God almighty, I've come at last!" Paul Smith thought of the janitor and smiled.

The dog's ancient eyes didn't even blink. "Won't you let me in, little piggy?" said Smith, but Simba failed to respond. Then the dog stepped back a pace, the eyes almost disappearing into shadow. Just two little lights remained. Paul Smith bent and picked up a softball-sized stone near the bottom of the steps. "Never was a lock picker, Simba, and I don't really have time. I have to get back to Debra. My wife, you see. She pines when I'm away. Not like Digger's. Digger's wife left him, did you know that?"

At the name, Simba's tail wagged, a bit reluctantly, and she stepped back another pace, said "Woof."

Smith tapped the rock against the glass near the door knob, and on the third bump, a bit more forceful, the pane gave way and shards tinkled to the kitchen floor. The tall man used the stone to clear away some broken glass, then lowered his head to the paperback-sized opening, looked in at Simba with one bloodshot eye, said "Boo!" Simba stepped back again, then again, and left the kitchen.

The man put his hand through the broken entranceway, carefully, and unlocked the back door, fingers stretching and latching onto the knob like an octopus. As the sun began its hidden descent in earnest, Paul Smith entered Digger's house and pushed the broken glass out the door onto the top step. *Must tidy up!* Simba was gone, and the cottage failed to greet him. "Not a particularly happy home," said Smith, and then he called for Simba: "Here, doggie, here, doggie. Be a good dog and come to Uncle Paul."

Simba didn't appear, so the man walked from the little living room down the little hall. "Everything's little in here," he said aloud happily. He opened the front door a foot or so. He looked at his ugly old car. *Who drives a station wagon? Looks like an old tank. I'll just leave it here when I go.* "Here, Simba. Here, Simba!"

Simba poked her head out of a doorway off the living room. *Must be Digger's bedroom.* "We have to offer Digger a nice welcoming homecoming, don't we, Simba?"

At the question, Simba cocked her head and then stepped toward the interloper, who felt a ripple of fear down his back. The dog just looked so wild, so present and capable. From his sweatshirt's front pocket, Paul Smith, the composition instructor of over thirty years, extracted a long silver object. One edge was rippled and jagged, like big teeth. The man gave the dog a twisted smile. "My teeth are bigger than yours, Simba. Beautiful, isn't it? A present from my father, and from his to him. From Smith to Smith, Simba, just think of it! This blade has blazed in the trenches of France, gleamed on the islands of the Pacific!"

For a moment, the hooded man seemed lost in the past century, turning the big knife slowly, watching light ripple along the heavy steel.

Then Smith looked down at the motionless dog. "I would have answered the call, too, Simba, but no battles beckoned. Still, I polished this heirloom, and I have fed it, too. Why, we Smiths have been dealing with enemies for a hundred years."

Simba kept her eyes on the strange man, who stared back. Neither creature blinked.

Then the tall man took a two-legged step toward the short dog, who took a four-legged one back. Six legs in unison, four eyes locked.

Driving home from the police station, Digger felt both less and more afraid: less because he had acted, communicated; more because his words seemed to have made a hypothetical idea real, to have manifested a monster. The skies still imitated his mood, too, for the motionless, cavernous gloom continued to hang over Ocean View, a heavy woolen blanket, a smothered breath held against the earth. Digger liked clouds, but not this thick air, and when he reached his driveway, he received a shock: a visitor in the form of an old station wagon, the type with faux-wood paneled siding—a rare form of transport after the millennium. He had seen that old car before (where?), but at the moment it was empty. Suddenly his thoughts funneled into a single fear: "Simba!" And hearing a high-pitched bark, he sprinted to his door.

It yawned open about a foot, and now Digger remembered the car, which he had noticed in the faculty parking lot a few times, and he remembered the driver, too, having seen him lumber off in that relic to the 70's and 80's more than once. Paul Smith was here, in his cottage, with Simba.

Digger thought immediately of Doyle, of retracing his steps to his little truck and returning to the police station, and then of Simba again—of Simba. Fear of loss ignited Digger's little pilot light of a life into a burning torch. He entered his home immediately and called out, "Hello! Paul? Is that your car? Simba?"

Paul appeared, coming around the corner from the kitchen, hands by his side, wearing a hooded sweatshirt. *Where was Simba?* Hooded, the thin face looked both younger and older, and Digger thought illogically of a pistachio nut, of the green meat peering from its shell.

"Hello, Digger," said the nut. "Your door was open. You should lock your door, you know. Someone could come in and take your dog. You don't seem to have any other valuables"

"Simba!" said Digger, stepping forward. "Simba!"

"He's fine," said Paul. "I put him in that back room because I want to talk with you. I want to talk, Digger. Let's talk."

Despite the situation, Digger felt annoyed that Paul called Simba "him," so he corrected the probable killer, saying "Simba's female," and then "Okay, let's talk." Digger could in fact hear Simba now. She was scratching at his bedroom door and woofing repeatedly in her muffled, grunting way. Digger felt a deep stab of relief and love for his dog.

"Let's talk in the kitchen," he volunteered, and Paul simply turned around and disappeared into the kitchen. Digger contemplated lunging for his bedroom door and barricading himself behind it with Simba, but instead he hurried after his odd colleague (to keep him in sight) and found the other man seated at the small kitchen table. Despite the presence of another person—or perhaps because of it—the room seemed emptier than usual. Smith seemed completely at ease, and Digger saw no knives or other weapons. He seated himself opposite Paul Smith. An odor reached his nostrils, and he thought immediately of Simba—had this man hurt her? Then he remembered Simba's woofing and scratching, as well as Paul Smith's recent grooming deficiencies. Feeling close to a conclusion, Digger actually settled into his chair, for while sitting two yards from a killer (most likely, anyway), he now felt oddly calm, peaceful, ready. The two men could be about to commence a game of chess. From outside, Digger heard a gull eayut-yut-yutting off into the sea.

"How can you stand those birds' noises?" said Paul Smith, his first move laced with bitterness. "They scream all day at school, and you come home to them screaming all the rest of the time. Nothing else around here seems to make a noise. Your house seems like a tomb, Digger."

"I like gulls," said Digger. "They're timeless."

"Timeless?" spat Smith. "Time is time, and we can't escape it. Whatever happens in time happens, and then time goes on, regardless and uncaring. There's always a time. Even in this tomb, Digger."

Digger had hated time like this seven and a half years ago, still did on occasion, so the bitter soliloquy had no real effect other than to puzzle him. The other's "tomb" references were obviously meant to needle him, so he ignored them. "Paul, are you okay? You seem a bit agitated. Would you like something to drink? Some coffee, maybe?"

"I have found that coffee tends to agitate me even more, especially at night. Coffee keeps me up all night. Do you know how that feels, Digger?"

Digger said that he did, and Paul Smith responded, "That's right, you would. Your wife ran out on you. I can imagine all those sleepless nights. Would she return? Would you want her to? Would you take her back? Even after she had been with another man? Or would you do something more ... drastic?"

"I would have taken her back," said Digger, surprising himself. "I still would, but Anna won't come back. I know that now. I've known it for years."

Paul Smith seemed not to know what to say to that; he just stared at Digger, no expression on either man's face. Simba said, "Woof!"

"Woof!" repeated the bitter and hooded man. "That about sums it all up, doesn't it? Dogs are so much smarter and more consistent than people, don't you think?" Digger nodded; he did think.

"We're better off now, Digger," Paul said, switching gears and tactics. "Don gave me a great spring schedule, three classes! One of Tobias,' too, since all four of his were now up for grabs. Isn't that funny? Pinsky the idiot would gloat about punishment from above, but I received an extra class. You see, Don valued experience, and loyalty. Tobias, he didn't value experience or loyalty, Digger. He just cared about appearances, about making the administration happy, and about females, about making them happy, the foolish old Casanova. We're better off with Don than with that old letch, don't you think?"

Digger thought of Elena, but he kept that story to himself. Then Paul continued, "And Pinsky, that blabbering janitor— well, it's better that his mouth is shut. And God no longer haunts our offices, Digger. I don't know who the janitor is now. Have they all been frightened off? I never see anyone with a mop anymore."

"They work a different schedule now," said Digger, thinking, thinking, for Paul Smith had just basically confessed to two murders and Digger wanted to get out, with Simba, and to contact Doyle—what would the little detective have advised right now? *Keep talking; keep the perpetrator distracted with words. Use his name, too.* Digger said of the maintenance crew, "They work during the day now, Paul. I'm surprised you don't see them in the morning."

"They must do our offices while I'm in class," replied Smith, still with no expression, but then he smiled: "They probably work pretty quickly on the Humanities corridor."

Digger decided to agree with everything Paul said. "I'm sure they do, Paul."

Smith paused again, but then continued on another tact. "I would take care of your dog, Digger. If anything happened to you."

"I know you would, Paul. I know that you're … loyal."

"I am loyal," repeated Paul Smith and then he laughed again, that quick bark, almost a cough. "Debra," he said, but he didn't add to that thought. Instead, he pushed the chair back, stood up, and just glared at Digger from across the table. Digger noticed the big knife now and thought, *he was sitting on it; that's where it was.* The knife looked huge as it hung from the end of Paul's arm, and then it gleamed somehow, a silver smile. It looked like the sort of weapon a soldier would take when sneaking up on the enemy to cut his throat.

Standing slowly, Digger imagined that same knife going into Tobias' back and almost through the man, of the plunge it took into Dan the Man, whose body was too big for the knife but not big enough to save him. Digger looked at death, and everything was still, quiet, even Simba, even the gulls, the sea.

"I'm sorry about this," said Paul Smith, and he did sound sort of sad. He began to move around the kitchen table. "But you think too much, Digger. You think and you talk, and you know the *Single-Stroke Killer*. You figured it out. You forced me to come here." As Paul moved, so did Digger—step, step; step, step. Ludicrously, Digger thought of a waltz, the squareness of their movements. He almost laughed. He felt buoyant, having come to an end of sorts.

"We need to stop dancing like this, Digger. I need to get home to Debra. She's always waiting for me at home."

Ah, Debbie, remembered Digger, and from the other room came that loud bark, high pitched, frantic, a Simba sound that Digger had never heard until just a few minutes earlier from the driveway. Inside, the sound rang much louder. It was a warning, a message of love, of desperation. The sound echoed forth again and again, giving Digger purpose and strength.

Paul Smith glanced out the door toward the sound, which made him flinch repeatedly. "That's a smart dog," he said, frowning. "I'm not sure I'll be able to take him, Digger. He might not like me too much after this. And he barks way too much. I can't stand dogs that bark."

Anger blossomed now in Digger, not because the man across from him wanted to kill him, but because of Simba, the unfair summation of his dog, the disregard of her proper gender. "Simba's not a 'he,' and she doesn't bark too much," he declared, louder than before. "She's barking because of you. If you get the hell out of here, she'll stop barking. You're the one causing the noise, Paul. Simba can't stand you!"

Paul Smith took in the words, which caused his body to freeze, his eyes to narrow a bit. Then the hooded man smiled horribly, revealing the black gap, and said, "Why, Digger, I do believe that you love that dog. She's replaced your darling run-away wife."

"Who do you love, Paul? Anyone? What would Debbie say about your little side jobs? Does she know that you're a killer?"

The name of his wife struck a mark, wiped the leer from Smith's face, but then the unbalanced grin returned, sort of. "Whom, Digger, the word is 'whom.' And, yes, Debra knows, and she understands. She stayed with me, Digger. How does that feel? You wouldn't know, would you? Your wife ran away from you."

Digger's anger had congealed, solidified, become a wall, so the taunts about Anna did nothing to him, just bounced off. He heard Simba woofing and crying and scratching. He had to escape for her sake, for her sake and for his. Simultaneously, the two men started to move again, back and forth, step, step; step, step. *The last waltz*, Digger thought, and now he was facing the window again, facing the sea. A red cardinal flitted past the window, the microwave announced 6:38 in blue numbers, and Digger realized that night had come.

Digger tried to slow the other's pace. "Why, Paul? Why did you do it?"

The other man laughed. "Why not? Tobias was a despot, Pinsky an idiot. Why not? Debra agreed, and I've always wanted to, always felt the desire to use this knife, my father's knife. He called it our Smith and Lesson. Get it, Digger? Smith and Lesson?"

Digger's mind slowed and focused. He noted the broken pane of glass in his own back door and thought, "I'll need some putty for that." Then his mind shifted back to the other, to the immediate problem. "Smith and Lesson," he said. "Well, my father gave me a Smith and Wesson, and if you don't leave I'll get it and shoot you, Paul. I won't hesitate to use it."

Paul Smith wasn't listening to the present, just turning the big knife slowly as though seeing scenes in the blade, memories. "Handed down to me," he murmured to himself. "Used in the wars, the great wars." He awakened and stared straight into Digger's eyes. "A family heirloom, Digger, and those are important, not to be locked away. And of course, Debra, we would do anything for our wives!"

"You killed Tobias for your wife?" *Keep him talking*, the little detective would have advised. *Keep him preoccupied.*

Smith gazed at the saw-like knife and then pulled his eyes from it to Digger's. "Don't you ever feel wild, Digger? Like you have to let the wild out?"

"No," answered Digger, and then he surprised himself by letting the truth out. "I feel broken, Paul, felt broken, but I don't feel that way anymore."

"You don't? Why not?" As he asked, the man with the weapon actually cocked his head, reminding Digger of Simba's questioning stare, and he almost chuckled at death.

"I think it was you, Paul. You reminded me that life is good, worth living. You saved me, Paul." And Digger realized that he was not just casting words to ensnare, that what he had said was true.

"Okay, Professor Diggerson, if you say so," said the hooded man, and his head cocked back straight, the sliver of wrinkled face like an old notched hatchet. "Well, if I can save you, I can also sacrifice you, right? And your little dog, too, your little dog, too, Digger, ha, ha, ha …"

Digger suddenly wanted to jump across the table and smash the other man, simply pummel him into rags, but he knew that Paul was baiting him, evoking dark pathos, coaxing him into a fatal move, into knife space. Digger stood a bit crouched and gave the other not a flinch.

What about Debra? When he mentioned her, Smith leaked a little, Digger realized, and he wondered whether Debra was actually part of the killings, a participant, and thought that Paul Smith needed to be locked away, but since at present he knew no way of getting it done, he started to ask about Debra when Smith lunged, the knife circling past and dividing the space before Digger, cutting nothing but air, a fact that seemed to enrage the sinewy and sinister Smith, who began to scramble around the table, like a big crab, a mad creature with one big pincher, snapping. Digger shuffled madly for his life, too.

The dance had begun in earnest. Gaining a step, Smith swung the grey death down, but Digger—fast for a middle-aged guy who did no cardio exercises (besides walking with Simba)—sprang back and twisted so that the knife nearly missed him completely, just nicked his left shoulder, which unbeknownst to Digger, started to bleed, trickle. In a frenzy now, Smith pushed forward like a focused and famished bear, hoisting the knife (the great claw) up again, slashing, up and down, scrambling around so that Digger had to mirror the dance as closely as possible, keeping the table between the actors as best he could. But Smith finally realized that the table was just a table, and not a particularly large one at that, so the Bear flung it away with one hand and lunged forward with the other, the knife hand, which passed over Digger's back because Digger had reacted offensively for the first time, ducking and launching himself forward. The two bodies met with a thud that Digger felt but didn't hear, because his ears rang with adrenaline, with crashing waves, with Simba's repeated lament, and with an echoing word because Digger had been here before, had felt the knife, knew the feel of its cold piercing snout, had died already, died and risen, again and again. *Anna, Anna, Anna!* The sounds broke out of his ears and mingled with a reverberating howl that had to be Simba, but could have been anybody, anything, a whistling tear in time.

Digger held Smith's knife arm up, frozen in the moment, but the Bear seemed to be stronger, madly powerful, the knife slowly lowering, down, down, a gleaming descent. Digger no longer recognized conscious thoughts. Images assailed him like a film running wild, each screen registering and then leaping to the next: Anna's face (her sweet profile), Anna's words ("I'm not happy"), steel words becoming a steel stiletto ("free!"), a silver slash, the Bear's face, teeth and intention. And Digger realized that he *had* been here before, in this kitchen, stabbed long ago and left for dead, and now it was happening again, happening for real, for this time it was real. *Not this time! Not Simba!* Jabbing his left leg behind Paul Smith, he pushed the Bear, tripped it, landed on top of the frenzied creature, still keeping the knife at bay above their heads. And Digger held it there as the killer's body twisted beneath him, as the waves crashed in his ears, which echoed with that single pulsing word: *Anna, Anna, Anna!* And then the knife inched down, just inches above Digger's head, and suddenly Digger realized that Anna was not just a word in his head but one that flew and crashed around the room, a seagull's scream of fear and fury, a manic tune to the howling base of Simba's song of sorrow. And the rebounding layers of sound startled the Bear, who (alone against all these life forces) really didn't have a chance now, who was half dead already but didn't know it. The stiffly raised knife arm went soft for an instant, and in that moment Digger jammed his right knee into the other's crotch, and Paul Smith let out a crushing moan and curled up beneath Digger, dropping his father's family heirloom, rolling and twisting and whispering, "Oh, oh, oh…"

Digger did not hesitate. He sprang up, spry for a middle-aged guy, rushed through the doorway to his bedroom door, which he pulled open to reveal Simba, her eyes wide, her mouth wide, her tail a blur. The inside door showed deep scratches, trails of blood that looked dark in the shadowed room. "Come on, Simba!" he called, and Simba did it, right out the open front door, right into the pickup (with a little hoist from Digger), right out the driveway and down the street. As his truck's headlights blazed a path through the falling night, Digger thought, *Anna, Anna,* the waves in his ears still crashing, but softening now, almost a melody.

It was the song of Anna, Digger realized: the gift of life, of freedom. He understood now that this visceral call to the past had not been unleashed to cling or call Anna back, but to cast her off, to let her go.

The little detective caught up with Paul Smith in less than an hour. Within twenty minutes, the Massachusetts State Police spotted the old station wagon's license plate on 195 East, heading toward Cape Cod. With sirens and lights blaring, the cops chased the old vehicle for a couple miles, both cars pushing 80, but then Smith pulled off the highway and exited his vintage vehicle, which wheezed and died. His descent into the moon's shadows ended there beneath the purplish twilight of a mid- to late-March evening, the stars leaking love and hopeless futures, just as Digger used to do. Held within the police car's spotlight, Smith raised up his hands to those stars, keys in one grip, no knife in either. Smith had pulled the hood down from his face, which looked lined and lost. He offered no resistance, no words at all. No wind was left beneath the Condor's wings, no fight pulsing in the Bear, no howl left in the Wolf or the Fox. The wild had been caged. It had been defeated by a man who loved a dog and a woman who went away, a broken man who fought for life.

No knife appeared in the car, either, but after he arrived on the scene, Detective Doyle had a hunch: from the side of 195 East, with Paul Smith slouched in the back of his SUV, Doyle called the station and ordered divers to Digger's beach. Already, however, the waves had spat back the silver tool that had recently taken two lives, wanting two others, a man and his dog. With their powerful flashlights, the dry divers spotted the weapon almost as soon as they stepped on the beach. Gleaming but ugly, with serrated teeth: the jaw of a monster tossed up by the sea after its symbolic deliverance by an old man with nothing left but a family heirloom and a misguided sense of purpose.

At Smith's house, Doyle and his peers found another body—
—Debra Smith's, dead for months, left propped up in a swayback chair in a back room. The woman was not a pretty sight (and not pleasant to the olfactory system, either), but Paul Smith had not killed his wife, not that the pathologist could tell. Life had done that, a coronary, one that had taken two hearts, then two others.

Two days after all the activity—the cops, the reporters, the concerned friends, his mother, his aunts, even strangers— Digger's home phone sounded again for at least the twentieth time (ten by his mother alone), but Digger answered them all. His bout with a killer had changed him, made him realize that he wanted to live, that he could exist, even alone. After all these years, Digger now understood why Anna had used the word "free," for now he felt that way: free of baggage, free of himself. Even a ringing phone sounded happy. Digger snatched up the handle.

"It's me," came a nearly forgotten voice. "I read the paper about the murders, about you. I've been keeping track since the first one when I saw the name Ocean View College. It's all horrible." She didn't explain "it," but Digger knew.

"It's been unreal," he replied, surprised that his heart beat normally, that his thoughts and voice were clear. "How are you, Anna?"

She laughed at that, a breezy sound, summer winds. "How am I? I'm fine. Nobody's tried to kill me. But what about you? How are you?"

"I'm fine, too," Digger realized and then said, and they talked for a long time, two souls who had once sung the same song, first about his life, then about hers. With his eye on a sleeping dog that looked a bit like a lion, Digger sat and enjoyed the conversation, which contained no agendas, no crashing waves, no howling winds, no screaming gulls, no expectations, no passive aggression, no words blackly masked and mashed. When they said goodbye, Digger didn't even ask for her number, didn't even request that they "get together" or speak again, that they connect, sew together the years, the wounds.

"Good bye, Anna," Digger said into the phone before cradling it. Later that day, he took a trip to the Ocean View Pound to find Simba a sister, for should any home have just one dog?

THE END

ABOUT THE AUTHOR

After graduating from the University of Connecticut and then Arizona, Dave returned to New England to teach college composition and continues to do so. In Providence, Rhode Island, he lives happily with his wife (Elena) and two dogs (Belle and Holly). His "Simba" passed away peacefully in 2013 at the age of 16.

Made in the USA
Middletown, DE
09 July 2017